CW00673767

THE
UNLIKELY COWBOY

A Flat Top Mountain Adventure

JAMES E. DOUCETTE

The Unlikely Cowboy
A Flat Top Mountain Adventure
James E. Doucette © 2021

This book is a work of fiction. While some of the people, places, and names are real, details may be changed for the purpose of enhancing the story.

Softcover ISBN: 978-1-7340498-4-8
eBook ISBN: 978-1-7340498-5-5

Available as softcover and ebook at online retailers, including Amazon.com

Published by James E. Doucette

Printed in the United States of America

This book is dedicated to my wife and partner, Denise.

"This Is Dedicated to the One I Love."

—the Supremes

AUTHOR'S NOTES

This book is a work of fiction and is not autobiographical. It is, however, based on real life characteristics of people I admire and actual locations.

Kenneth Wyatt, the famous West Texas artist, is not a fictional character, and he is mentioned several times in *The Unlikely Cowboy*. I was writing this book when Kenneth Wyatt passed away. Over the years, Denise and I visited his gallery several times; when he was in town, he talked with visitors. One day I was looking for a unique gift for my cousin, who lived by the shore in south New Jersey. I noticed a beautiful painting of a sailing ship sitting among the cowboy art, religious renderings, and sculptures.

I was looking at the picture, and Kenneth walked over. I asked, "Why did you paint a sailing ship?"

He smiled and told me, "I served in the merchant marines." Add that to his impressive list of occupations: a cowboy, poet, sculptor, bricklayer—he helped my pastor, Tommy Beck, with a bricklaying project—and was a true "renaissance man."

When Denise and I built an addition to our house with a stone fireplace, we discussed what painting to place above the fireplace.

I said, "I'm going to call Kenneth Wyatt." After several minutes' conversation, I told him we owned the Flat Top Mountain Ranch and asked if he would do an oil painting of the mountain. He responded, "That's what I do for a living."

Kenneth graciously spent time with us at the ranch. We are the proud owners of a Kenneth Wyatt original titled, "Through the Gate." This painting is featured in the photo I used for the cover of my biography, published in 2015, *The Not So Great American Novel*. It's a photo of me standing under our one and only Kenneth Wyatt oil painting. Mr. Wyatt now has a broader canvas to paint on in heaven.

The Night Owl Café (known in real life as the Ghost Horse Gallery/Night Owl Espresso and Tea Bar) is located in Silverton, Texas. In *The Unlikely Cowboy*, I relocated it to Canyon, Texas, to work better with the plot. What I've written about the café I hope does it justice. Rowdy, the blind barista, is a real person who works at the Night Owl Espresso Bar—a fantastic individual. These ideas helped me create a background for the story. The other characters used in the Night Owl Café scenes are fictional. "Rowdy's" actual mother does not have a Boston accent.

The character of Megan, the lady who owns the raptors (birds of prey), was inspired by the real life artist Tammy L. Penn, whom I've never met. The backgrounds I've written for each character are from my imagination and not meant to disparage.

I wrote about the Bison Café, an actual restaurant located in Quitaque (pronounced "kit-a-kway"), Texas. I hope I've done it justice. They have a great menu and a wonderful gift shop. The chef creates hamburgers to die for. They also sell my books—yes, a shameless plug.

In the book, the gin I described was based on the D&J Cotton Gin, owned by Jody and David Foster. It is a fantastic operation and adds vitality to Lockney, Texas. Their families have owned and operated the gin for as long as I can remember; I've lived here for thirty-five years. I had the privilege of calling the Fosters' grandfather, J.R. Belt, my friend.

The welcoming, friendly atmospheres I have portrayed in the small Texas towns featured in the book are real. If you would like to experience them for yourself, here's my suggested tour: Start at Tulia, Texas, with a visit to the Wyatt studio. Next, drive to Silverton and visit the Night Owl/Espresso and Tea bar. The chai latte is my favorite, along with a bowl of homemade ice cream.

Next, stop in Quitaque for lunch at the Bison Café, stroll Main Street, and stop at the Coffee Mill and Mercantile—they have exquisite local crafts and great sandwiches and snacks.

Next, drive up to Caprock Canyons State Park and see the herd of bison that are descended from Charles Goodnight's original herd. Goodnight started this herd in 1878 in an effort to save the animals from extinction. Then, exit the park and go south on FM 1065 to FM 97. Here, the Flat

Top Mountain Ranch dominates the valley. Denise and I are delighted to have visitors. The only limitations are that you must have a pickup to handle the roads, the time, and the good luck to have favorable weather conditions. My random lower back pain might be an issue too. My email address is james_doucette@yahoo.com.

I chose the city of Canyon (its real name) as the backdrop for the book due to its proximity to the areas where the story's action takes place. It's a city worth visiting. The town has several shops and galleries that surround the square. Unfortunately, the courthouse building is, in truth, not in use. While in Canyon, visit the Panhandle-Plains Historical Museum, and no trip to the area would be complete without exploring Palo Duro Canyon State Park.

Chapter 1

START OF ANOTHER DAY

The 81st Precinct, Brooklyn, New York – August 14, 2015

Sergeant Joseph D'Angelo entered the squad room at 8 a.m., as he'd been doing for twenty years.

Officer Brush was the first to greet him. "Good morning, Sarge." All the officers under Joe's command called him Sarge or Sergeant Joe.

It's young men like this one who make life worthwhile, Joe thought as he nodded and smiled. He stopped at the front desk to talk to his old partner, Sergeant Henry. The desk sergeant had been injured on the job and assigned to light duty. "How's the hip today?"

"Ready to challenge you to a foot race!" Henry smiled and said, "Well, maybe not today."

Joe remarked, "We had some great years together on patrol."

Henry nodded. "We sure did. This injury could have been worse if it weren't for you."

"We were partners."

"We still are. Have a great day."

Joe continued down the hallway toward the breakroom. His light olive skin and Roman nose were proof of his family's Mediterranean heritage. His dark hair with streaks of gray accentuated his manly face. He stood five feet, ten inches tall and carried the same 160 pounds of weight he had in the Army.

Every morning before he left for the precinct, he did weight training followed by a three-mile run. During his run, he thought about the day ahead. It helped him clear his head.

This morning, his thoughts had been on the past. The last few years had not been kind to him. In 2010 his mother and father passed away. His mother died in June, and his father gave up the will to live and passed away in September. Joe's wife, Anna, succumbed to cancer in 2012, and his only son was killed in action in 2013.

At the memorial service for his son, the priest told the mourners that the Lord never gives you more than you can handle. The same priest had married Joe and Anna, baptized their son, and buried his wife and parents.

As the graveside service ended, the priest turned to Joe. "Your burden is something I can't imagine."

Joe had looked down and shook his head. "It makes no sense."

"Is there anything I can do to help?"

"I have my faith, my job, and a few friends. I'll be okay. I appreciate your offer."

As the men parted company, the priest said a silent prayer for Joseph D'Angelo.

On his way to his desk, Joe glanced into the breakroom and saw Officer Eddie Brush holding court—that guy sure did like to tell stories. It wasn't enough that he was a senior officer and good-looking enough to get more than his share of dates; he had to let everyone know Joe picked him as his partner more times than not, and he was proud of it. That, and the guys couldn't seem to get enough of the stories Brush told them about Joe, even if they made him seem a little larger than life.

Joe wasn't comfortable being painted a hero, but there wasn't a lot he could do to stop Brush—and sometimes he didn't want to. Joe stood outside the breakroom as Brush's words filled the room.

"You should have seen the sarge take down a perp running out of a bodega. He jumped out of the patrol car when he saw a six-foot Hispanic running out of the store. The sarge yelled, 'Stop.' That yell could stop a freight train. The frightened perp's hands trembled as he tried to draw a .38 from his waistband." The men were spellbound.

"It looked like Sarge's hand moved quicker than lightning; in less than a second, the perp was on the ground, screaming.

"He looked at me and said, 'Would you mind cuffing this kid? I didn't break his arm.' As I was cuffing the guy, he asked the store owner, 'Que pasa, Luis?'

"The store owner pointed to the cuffed perp and screamed in Spanish. The sarge held up his hand and said, 'Luis, speak English.'

13

"The store owner said, 'He emptied my register of about $300.'

"Sarge helped the owner get the criminal up and empty his pockets. We found a wad of cash and a wallet. Sarge counted the money and said, 'Looks like it's all here.' He handed the money back to the store owner. The sergeant walked to our patrol car with the robber's wallet. When he returned, I said, 'Don't we need that money as evidence?'

"Sarge ignored me and grabbed the perp's arm and twisted just a bit and asked, 'You know you have the right to have an attorney present, don't you?' The guy nodded. Sarge said, 'Say it out loud.' The guy finally said, 'Yes.'

"Sarge then told the guy, 'We're going to take you in and book you for attempted robbery. But unfortunately, the pistol is going into the river. So at most, you'll get a year in prison.'

"The perp looked confused, so Sarge had to explain. 'If I book you for possession of a firearm, you'll get an immediate five-year sentence.'

"The store owner, looked at the perp and said, 'Sergeant Joe is giving you a break; make the most of it.'

"As we drove away, I asked Sarge, 'How did you know the perp wasn't going to shoot you?'

"Sarge said, 'Pros have shot at me. Always be aware of the situation and act appropriately. I know everyone calls us police officers, but I like to think I'm a peace officer.'"

The story ended as D'Angelo walked into the squad room. "Attention to orders."

The twenty police officers in the squad room quieted, all eyes focused on Sergeant D'Angelo. "Today will be challenging. Temperatures are going to reach 95 degrees, and the humidity will match the heat." He made eye contact with each officer. "Be careful out there. Dismissed." The officers paired up as they exited the squad room.

"Officer Brush, you're riding with me. Get our gear and meet me at my patrol car." Joe liked to ride with Brush.

"Roger that, Seargent."

It was department policy for the sergeant to report to the precinct captain at the beginning of a shift. Joe knocked on the door, entered, stood at attention, and saluted. "Sir, the squad is all present and accounted for and has been dispatched. I'm riding patrol with Officer Brush."

Captain O'Connell didn't return the salute or look up from his paperwork. "Okay." O'Connell was a 30-year veteran of the NYPD. Years of desk duty had added inches to his waist. The only exercise he got was marching down Fifth Avenue in the annual St. Patrick's Day parade.

D'Angelo headed to his patrol car. Brush was stowing their equipment.

Brush said, "Ready to roll. Do you want me to drive?"

"Okay."

"Let's cruise down Broadway to Kings Highway. I want to see who's hiding out under the elevated line."

The Broadway elevated rail line was the primary commuter link to Manhattan; it ran from Kings Highway and crossed the Williamsburg Bridge. The train rode on derrick structures through Brooklyn, spewing soot and blackening the buildings facing the tracks. Little sunlight penetrated the dense latticework. As the trains exited the bridge, they entered a tunnel and became part of the New York City subway system.

Blind spots and noise provided a perfect cover for crime. Houses abutting the line vibrated with each passing train and made conversation impossible. Those who rode the trains were working-class people and targets for crooks and pickpockets. Their daily commute started and ended with swift passage through these dangerous areas. Street smarts were the only weapon unarmed commuters had.

Joe's eyes constantly surveyed the streets. "Pull over," he told Brush.

They stopped near one of Joe's favorite con artists. Cue Ball Kelly was a notorious hustler. "Cue Ball, you got any bathtub-made Chanel Number 5 in that suitcase?"

"Headed for Midtown Manhattan, Sergeant Joe. I don't make no sales in the 81st." His eyes lit up. "Maybe we could have a friendly game of eight-ball tonight?"

Joe smiled. "No, thanks. Where's Mike the Goon?"

"He's working Times Square."

"Have a nice day." Joe closed the window and motioned for Brush to drive on. "He's quite a character. If he spent half as much energy on legitimate business, he'd be a wealthy man."

"Sarge, have you ever played pool with Cue Ball Kelly?"

"Once."

Chapter 2

PABLO JIMENEZ

Juarez, Chihuahua, Mexico

For a cartel leader, Pablo Jimenez's office was sparse. His plain desk faced a bulletproof door. The shatterproof windows looked out on a walled courtyard topped with electrified razor wire. Two chairs sat in front of his desk. Pablo looked up when he heard a noise outside his door.

Chico entered. "Me mandaste a buscar?"

"Speak English. You need to practice."

"Yes, Boss."

Pablo leveled a cold eye on his subordinate. "I'm sending you to Canyon, Texas, to set up a distribution network. Pick two others to go with you. Our local banker there will handle all cash. We will begin shipping product in a month."

Chico survived the cartel wars by maintaining a low profile. Pablo thought, *My best men were killed in the war. I hope this moron will do as I've trained him.*

Chico's face lit up. "I'm ready."

Pablo's blank stare removed the smile from Chico's face. "We'll see." The cartel boss continued. "Here's an envelope with a burner phone and ten grand spending money. Our gringo at the border will pass you through customs." Pablo dismissed Chico with a wave of his hand.

Chico closed the door behind him and let out an audible sigh.

Pablo's secured cell phone buzzed. He answered in Spanish, "Hola, Abuela." His grandmother didn't speak English.

"I haven't heard from Hector. How is he?"

"Hector is doing okay, grandmother. I sent him to New York City to stay with a friend of mine."

"Why did you do that?"

"His life was in danger if he stayed in town." He didn't tell her that the other cartel leaders said they'd take out Hector because he was killing innocent civilians for no reason—it was bad for business. The only reason Hector wasn't dead was out of respect for Pablo.

His abuela, Senora Jimenez, was the widow of a notorious murdered drug dealer. She responded, "I curse your father's and grandfather's graves for getting you boys into the drug business."

Pablo sat in silence. His grandmother broke into tears.

He spoke gently. "Please don't cry. I'm working hard to get the family out of Papa's business."

"You come to dinner on Sunday, and we'll go to church."

"Yes, Grandmother."

Pablo had sent his children and Hector's children to a boarding school in Spain. His grandmother worshipped her grandchildren. Pablo's and his brother's girlfriends had fled the country during the drug wars. He didn't know where the women went and didn't want to know—he had enough people to worry about. *El Chapo was stupid to lead an extravagant lifestyle. I'm not going to make myself a target. If Hector behaves, we'll be ready to get out of this life in two years.*

Chapter 3

THE CALL TO ABUELA

Juarez, Chihuahua, Mexico

Hector Jimenez felt his cell phone vibrate; he looked at the phone's screen and murmured, "My brother—what does he want?"

Hector answered. "Hola, Pablo."

Pablo responded, "I was talking to Abuela and she asked about you. Why haven't you called her?"

"I've been busy. I'll call her later today."

Pablo asked, "Have you contacted my friend?" He already knew the answer.

"I'm getting ready to."

"What are you busy doing?"

"This and that."

"If you get in trouble up there, I can't cover for you."

"Don't worry."

"Call Abuela!"

The brothers ended the call as abruptly as they started it.

Hector thought, *When El Chapo ran the crew, I was his enforcer. Now my brother thinks he's going to take over. Pablo and his friends say my methods are too rough—they forget that my methods kept everyone in line.*

Hector was surprised at how easy it was to recruit followers. His dark wavy hair framed his masculine features. Years of weight lifting and situps had sculpted his five-foot-eight frame. His tattoos and diamond earring completed the picture of a drug dealer. Hanging out in a local pool room made it easy to meet the local youths. Many thought he looked like Julio Cesar Chavez, a famous Mexican boxer.

His adept use of the pool cue earned him money and fame with the local teenagers. One night, an eight-ball tournament drew large crowds. Hector passed out free samples of weed as he scooped up his winnings. It didn't take long to develop a following—his best source of customers from the high schools.

Like ripples in a pond, his network grew, but increasing sales was stripping him of cash. He knew he couldn't get money from Pablo. He'd lived in his brother's shadow all of his life; his plan to rob a local bank took shape when he walked into Roosevelt Savings. The relaxed atmosphere, friendly staff, and a guard that looked like he should be in a nursing home seemed like an easy target.

His dealer, Juan, had two regular customers, a couple of teenage high school girls. Hector watched as Juan, in his usual spot, waved at the two girls as they approached. Before they could get close, two teenage boys halted them and tried to pull them away from him.

That was the opportunity Hector was waiting for; he crossed the street behind the teenagers and signaled to Juan. Both drew pistols and blocked the students. It didn't take long to recruit the helpers he needed for the bank robbery. Willy Simmons Jr. and his friend were easy to intimidate.

His plan would give him the money he needed to expand his network of dealers. As he sat in his apartment watching soccer, he thought, *I'll show Pablo.*

It wasn't too late that evening as he dialed his grandmother. "Hola, Abuela."

She asked, "Hector, where are you?"

He explained why he had to leave Mexico. He didn't mention the real reason why he had to go. Hector could always make his grandmother believe him. He explained how he was starting a new business. "Abuela, the gringos like Mexican goods. All I do is import and sell Mexican belts, wallets, and cowboy boots." He paused and then said, "I'll make you proud."

After the call ended, his grandmother began saying the rosary. She knew he was lying to her, and she asked the Lord to look over Hector.

Chapter 4

STANDING ON THE CORNER

Brooklyn, New York

The two young men stood on the corner. Hector approached them. "It's time to rock and roll."

Junior, the taller of the two, remarked, "I don't know about this."

Junior thought, *How did I get involved with this? This Mexican dealer has made addicts out of half the school. If I do this, maybe he'll do what he says and stop selling drugs in our neighborhood. I've got to get Deja off these drugs before she ruins her life.*

His thoughts were interrupted by Hector. "Put these masks on." He gave each boy a .38 pistol. "Don't worry— they're not loaded. Just for show." Hector smiled. "After this, you won't see me again."

Junior and his friend walked with Hector to the entrance of the Roosevelt Savings Bank. Hector glanced up and down the street. "Okay, let's go."

★ ★ ★

Phil Mitchell closed his employee locker and examined his appearance in the mirror. His uniform was clean and pressed. He had followed the same ritual during his twenty-five years as a New York City police officer and for nearly twenty years as a bank guard.

Phil mused about the history of the bank where he worked and how things had changed. The Roosevelt Savings Bank first opened its doors in 1907. Its classical design and bronze entrance radiated strength and stability until the late 1950s; it was the center for commerce for the Bushwick and Bedford-Stuyvesant neighborhoods. However, its glory days had faded.

The bank's business center had always reminded him of Grand Central Station—massive and ornate. He thought, *Time to make my rounds*, as he entered the cathedral-like banking center.

Mrs. Hennessy, the head teller, greeted him, "Top of the morning, Egbert."

"And the rest of the day to you, Mrs. Souse."

They both chuckled, knowing that no one else knew they had adopted the names of the characters from W.C. Fields' movie *The Bank Dick*.

Phil had seen the neighborhood's population slide into poverty. Today's bank customers needed a place to cash their paychecks; having an account meant that their meager earnings would escape the extraordinary fees charged by payday lenders. He glanced at his watch and as he walked by the branch president's glass-enclosed office. "Time to open up, Mr. Sawyer?"

"Right on time as usual." Sawyer continued, "You've been doing this since I was a teller trainee—you don't have to call me Mr. Sawyer."

Phil smiled and headed for the front door. "You've earned it, sir." Phil thought, *What a fine young man. It seemed like yesterday when he started right out of college. How many years ago was that?*

He disarmed the alarm system and unlocked the large bronze doors. As he turned to go back inside the bank, Hector burst through the door and stuck his pistol behind Phil's ear.

"Just do what I say, old man, and nobody gets hurt."

Chapter 5

ROBBERY IN PROGRESS

An hour into their patrol, Joe received a call on his private line from the precinct's desk sergeant. "We've got a silent alarm from the Roosevelt Savings Bank on Gates Avenue."

Joe responded, "On my way—five minutes from the bank." He switched to the channel reserved for emergency communication with his squad. "This is D'Angelo; all patrols report your locations." As the units responded, D'Angelo issued instructions. "There's been a silent alarm received at the precinct from the Roosevelt Savings Bank on Gates Avenue. Do not use your sirens, lights only. I don't want to create a hostage situation."

He continued, "We'd better cut off traffic in front of the bank. The bank guard, Phil, knows what to do. Unit four: stop all traffic from Broadway going up Gates Avenue. Unit ten: stop traffic from Ralph Avenue down Gates Avenue. All other units converge on the bank and form a barricade. We'll catch the perps as they come out of the bank."

Eddie and Joe pulled up in front of the bank; three units joined them. The patrol cars at the intersections had halted traffic. D'Angelo motioned the officers into position. Three men wearing hoodies and clown masks ran out of the bank. They spied the policemen and froze.

A bullhorn amplified D'Angelo's voice. "We've got you surrounded. Kneel and place your hands behind your head, fingers laced!"

The robbers pivoted and tried to reenter the bank, but Phil, the security guard, locked the doors immediately after the thieves exited the bank. He viewed the scene from behind the bulletproof glass. Then he turned toward the customers and employees. "Everyone stay calm. The police have the robbers surrounded."

One of the robbers tugged at the metal-reinforced door.

Hector fired at the bank door. The bullet ricocheted, and one of the robbers howled in pain and fell to the sidewalk.

Joe implored, "This is over. Don't make this worse than it is. All you're facing is some jail time. Surrender and make it easy on yourselves."

He continued, "No harm will come to you if you give this up. Your partner's wounded. We'll take him to the hospital."

Hector leveled his pistol at Joe. Joe's reaction was automatic; he shot him dead in the center of his chest. Hector's lifeless body slumped to the ground. The wounded robber was clutching his shoulder. Joe leveled his aim at the remaining perp; he raised his hands over his head.

Joe yelled. "Secure the prisoners!"

Joe ran up the bank steps and his officers followed. Joe noticed a tattoo of three stars on the wrist of the dead robber.

He shouted, "Call an ambulance." He pulled the mask off of the tallest bank robber, and his eyes widened in shock. "What?"

Staring up at the man he recognized, tears ran down Junior's face. "Mister Joe, I'm sorry." Junior remembered meeting Joe when he was young. He would never forget the picture sitting on the fireplace in his parents' house of Joe and his father in U.S. Army uniforms.

As soon as the area was secure, Joe dialed his army buddy. Willy Simmons answered, "Joe, what's up?"

"Willy, you need to come to the 81st Precinct. We have Junior in custody."

"What?"

"He was arrested robbing the Roosevelt Savings Bank on Gates Avenue. We'll talk more when I see you."

Joe's trembling fingers finally pushed the button and disconnected the call. The adrenaline subsided, and his hands shook. Scenes from Panama, the Persian Gulf, and the Columbian jungles flashed in his mind. He thought, *I don't want to be responsible for the death of another person.*

Chapter 6

BACKLASH

The 81st Precinct, Brooklyn, New York

A small crowd gathered around the news van. Katy Sumrall, the on-air reporter, was busy setting up for an interview. The Reverend Clinton and his entourage elbowed their way toward her. She was glad to see the reverend—he was always good for a ratings-boosting statement.

She said to the camera man, "Make sure the camera is turned on." The camera man shook his head and responded with a grimace, "That only happened once."

She smiled. *If you had a brain, you'd be dangerous.* She motioned him to get in position for the interview.

They had been through this drill before. The reverend always wanted to be facing the camera.

She asked, "Reverend Clinton, do you know what happened here?"

"This is another example of police overreaction. One black teenager is dead, and another is wounded. There is no reason for this; these boys peacefully left the bank when the cops opened fire. I'm demanding a complete investigation by the civilian review board and asking the FBI to file federal charges for violation of the civil rights of these young victims." Katy nodded toward the pistol in the Hispanic man's hand. The reverend ignored her.

"Thank you, Reverend." She pivoted toward the camera, her expression grim. "This is Katy Sumrall; I'm at the scene of the shooting in front of the Roosevelt Savings Bank on Gates Avenue in Brooklyn. We'll return you to Chet in our studio."

"I'm Chet Long, KCTV, reporting on the shooting of two black teenagers in front of the Roosevelt Savings Bank in Brooklyn. Our Katy Sumrall is reporting live from the scene. We've tried to get in touch with Police Commissioner Donovan at One Police Plaza, but an aide stated that the incident is under investigation." Chet adjusted his pink-rimmed glasses and continued, "We've got more reports from the scene." A split screen appeared with Katy. "Katy, can you fill in our viewers on what's happening?"

"Thank you, Chet. Protestors have blocked the street. I tried to interview the precinct captain. He said he could not comment on an ongoing investigation."

The camera man motioned for the twenty protestors to bunch up behind Reverend Clinton. The crowd's screaming of "Justice now!" almost drowned out Katy.

"As you can see, the community is demanding justice. Unfortunately, the mob is growing as we speak. Back to you, Chet."

Chet picked up his cue. "The situation is tense."

Adjusting his glasses again, he continued, "Katy, if you can hear me, be careful and don't get hurt. I'm Chet Long, reporting on the racial incident in front of the Roosevelt Savings Bank in Bedford-Stuyvesant, Brooklyn. We'll now return to your regularly scheduled programming."

Katy had to step away from the noise to hear Morrie Schwartz, her producer. She pressed her earpiece deeper in her ear. "Please repeat your message."

His annoyed voice repeated what he just said. "Katy, pack up and head to Central Park. There's been a murder near the Zoo."

"Morrie, there's more to this story. I'd like to find out what the bank's security cameras showed. The dead guy is Hispanic and had a pistol in his hand."

"You've got enough footage for the noon news. Get moving."

Joe entered the precinct house. Sergeant Henry saw him, rolled his eyes, and said, "Report to Captain O'Connell." When Joe opened the captain's office door, he saw two detectives flanking O'Connell.

Without looking at Joe, the captain stated, "These detectives are from the commissioner's office; they'll take your statement. But, first, I have to ask you for your badge and revolver."

Joe took off his shield, withdrew his pistol from its holster, and placed them on the captain's desk.

One detective said, "And your ankle weapon."

Joe lifted his pant leg, removed his snub-nosed .38 from its leg holster, and set it on the desk. Joe turned to leave; one of the detectives barked, "Wait, we have to take your statement. Follow me to the interrogation room."

The three men left the captain's office, but Joe heard O'Connell mutter, "The Italians should stick to the sanitation department," as he walked away.

Chapter 7

COFFEE AND TEA

The Night Owl Café, Canyon, Texas

Mrs. Milstead smiled as she watched her son, Rowdy, prepare a latte for a customer. She smiled at her thoughts. *The blind barista's reputation has spread. People come at first out of curiosity and return for the excellent coffee drinks and Rowdy's infectious personality.*

Rowdy called out, "Mother, someone is opening the back door. It must be Megan; she's the only other person with a key."

Mrs. Milstead turned and smiled at the petite blond coming toward her. "Megan dear, come, sit and join me." Mrs. Milstead left Boston over 40 years ago but maintained her Boston accent and demeanor. Her silver hair was combed into a bun that sat behind her head. Her attractive face and smooth skin hid her age. The Brahmins in her hometown would be proud to hear her say, "Pahk the cah."

Megan sat at the round metal table on a ladder-backed chair. Her blond hair was stuffed under a cowboy hat. The hat shaded her blue eyes and firm chin. She smiled at the older woman.

"It's nice to see you."

Mrs. Milstead said, "Have a latte, and we'll talk awhile." Before Megan could answer, Mrs. Milstead called out, "Rowdy would you make lattes for us and one for yourself and join us?" Then she turned to Megan. "I haven't seen you in months. Is there anything bothering you?"

"No, ma'am. I've been busy." She didn't meet the older woman's eyes. Her untucked denim shirt hung loosely over a pair of blue jeans, her Ariat boots caked with mud.

Mrs. Milstead thought, *Something is bothering her.*

"What's occupying your time?" she asked.

"I've been busy training my new peregrine falcon. She's brilliant and has caught on fast." Megan continued, "That ranch I've leased needs a lot of work. The fences need repair, and the grass hasn't had fertilizer or weed killer applied for many years. So I've rented a tractor with a spreader. I've spent nearly every day on the tractor."

Rowdy placed two lattes on the table, went to the counter, fetched one for himself, and sat down. Rowdy turned toward Megan. "It's been a while since I've seen you—oops." His smile broadened. "You know what I mean."

Mrs. Milstead spoke, "The business is doing wonderful. We've hired a waitress to help serve the customers. I'm doing the baking."

Megan laughed, "I smell the cinnamon rolls—brings back happy memories."

Rowdy asked, "Have you met any interesting men?"

Megan frowned. "No!" Then she retorted, "What happened to your high school sweetheart?"

"None of your business!"

Mrs. Milstead thought, *It's been nearly three years since a carelessly thrown flashbang grenade blinded him. The DEA has healed him of his external scars but could not restore his sight or confidence.*

Mrs. Milstead raised her hand to stop Megan and touched Rowdy's arm. "Let's continue this discussion at another time."

The front door opened, and the bell tinkled. Rowdy stood. "I have a customer." Rowdy walked to the counter to greet the customer.

Mrs. Milstead gently touched Megan's hand. "Will you come to tea tomorrow?"

"Yes, ma'am."

Mrs. Milstead thought, *The children are having problems—and tea settles all troubles.*

Megan excused herself and left through the rear door.

Chapter 8

A FRIEND'S VOICE

Joe D'Angelo's home in Bensonhurst, Brooklyn

Joe looked around his living room. His wife, gone for three years now, had decorated the walls with memories. The furniture sat where she had placed it. Next to the fireplace was a picture of Joseph Jr. and Joe at Rockaway Beach, playing catch with a football. Square shadow boxes with wartime metals sat next to his police decorations. He stared at his pistol on the coffee table.

His cell phone chime startled him. "Hello?"

"Hey Sarge, it's Kyle Mitchell, your old army buddy."

Joe took a few seconds to placc the voice. "Hey, Kyle! What's up?"

"Old buddy, you made the news. I couldn't believe what I heard. I know you wouldn't have shot that crook for no reason." Kyle paused. "What's going on?"

"Every move the police make lately turns into a racial incident."

Kyle sighed. "That's ridiculous. Half our platoon was black or Hispanic." He continued, "How's your pretty wife and son? The boy's got to be around twenty."

Joe's voice broke, and he blurted out, "My wife died of cancer three years ago, and my boy was killed in action."

"Joe, why didn't you call me?"

"Didn't want to bother you."

"What?"

When Joe told him he arrested Willy Simmons' son, Kyle said, "It sounds like you're going through a world of hurt. Just hang on; I'm catching the next flight to New York."

Chapter 9

TIME TO THINK

The following day, Joe's cell phone woke him from a restless sleep. "This is Captain O'Connell. Report to my office as soon as you can." Before Joe could respond, the captain disconnected.

Joe took the familiar path to the 81st precinct and parked behind the station. He entered through the rear door. The entrance led past the detective's squad room and as Joe passed, the desk jockeys avoided eye contact and turned away. He knocked on the captain's door.

O'Connell barked, "Come in."

Joe noticed his badge and pistols sitting on the captain's desk. "You've created a storm of criticism. The commissioner's assistant called and told me to place you on administrative leave until the investigation is complete."

"Did you talk to the officers on the scene? Did you get the bank's surveillance tapes?"

"I can't discuss that. You'd better contact your union representative. That's all."

★ ★ ★

Joe spent another sleepless night. The next morning, he kept looking at the loaded pistol sitting on the coffee table. He shook his head and thought, *I've got to get out of here.*

He changed into his gym clothes and put on his running shoes. As he was leaving the house, an Uber cab pulled up. Kyle exited the car, grinning at his friend.

"I ain't jogging with you," Kyle said, rubbing his generous belly. His blond hair was thinning, but his boyish good looks told the world that his hair loss was premature. He still had a twinkle in his eye that promised mischief. He dropped his bag; his arms surrounded his old friend. "Let me drop off my bag, and we'll walk a spell." His West Texas accent brought a smile to Joe's face.

"Just the way I remember you, plus 30 pounds."

Kyle's eyes lit up. "Bet I can still beat you in arm wrestling!"

"No, thanks."

The men entered Joe's house. Kyle dropped his bag. "Let's walk."

The old friends spent the morning walking the footpath along the river toward downtown Brooklyn. They stopped at a grocery store and bought coffee and bagels. Joe opened up and told his old friend how killing a bank robber tormented him and that he arrested Willy Simmons' son. All Kyle could do was nod.

That night Joe told Kyle, "I have to visit Willy tomorrow."

Unsmiling, Kyle responded, "I'm coming with you!" The emphatic statement allowed no objection.

Kyle stayed by his side and insisted that Joe lock up his pistol. After breakfast in the Sixth Street Diner, Joe headed for his car. Kyle asked, "Where are we going?"

"To visit Willy."

Joe drove to Willy's brownstone house in Bedford-Stuyvesant, Brooklyn.

Willy opened the door. He glared at Joe and asked, "What do you want?"

As Willy readied to punch Joe, Kyle stepped between his two friends. Kyle's arms surrounded Willy. "Willy, it's me, Kyle. Please listen to me." The two men struggled. No matter how he tried, Kyle would not let him go. Finally, Willy exhaled and stated, "I'm okay. I know Joe was doing his job, but . . . "

Kyle responded, "But what? The boy had a mask on."

The three men had served together in the Army. Joe and Willy grew up in the same neighborhood and had enlisted in the U.S. Army at the same time. On the first day of Ranger training, the two met Kyle. During training, the three soldiers shared the hardships of training. While the other Ranger trainees complained, the trio made a joke of besting each other. Their deployments cemented their bonds.

Willy stated, "I need time to think."

Joe acknowledged, "We both do."

Chapter 10

THE NEIGHBORHOOD'S CHANGED

Back at home, Joe parked the car. Kyle stepped out and looked around. "This street has changed. When I visited your folks while we were on leave, this street was teaming with life. It reminded me of a village in Italy."

Joe nodded. "The neighborhood's become gentrified. Young people can't afford the rents in Manhattan. At seven in the morning, they rush to the Manhattan buses, and at night they come home with takeout meals. Their children are either at daycare or with a nanny."

"Pardner, I think this place has left you behind."

"I know."

"Let's drink some whiskey and talk about it."

Kyle opened the conversation. "Do you still repair rifles and pistols?"

"That's what I do to relax. I take care of most of the firearms in my precinct."

"You know my Texas buddies still talk about how you whipped their rifles into shape. A couple of them asked when you were coming back."

Joe smiled. "The Texans know how to shoot, but caring for firearms is foreign to them."

The conversation drifted to Joe's thoughts about his job. Joe told Kyle, "I've got enough time on the job to retire with a good pension. The Veterans Administration awarded me a thirty percent disability pension. There's also a fund for the people who worked at the World Trade Center after 9/11."

Kyle said, "Our town is in sore need of a gun repair shop. Maybe you should give it a try?"

"That's a big move."

"No, it ain't. Take away the houses, trees, mountains, rain, and people, and this place is just like Canyon, Texas."

Joe laughed. "I remember saying about the same thing in reverse when I visited Canyon—you need new material."

Kyle poured more whiskey. "And another drink."

The following day, Joe didn't awake until 10. Kyle greeted Joe with a cup of coffee. "I think we made a plan last night. How does it look in daylight?"

Joe smiled. "I've got to think about this."

Kyle's eyes flashed mischief. "What-ta you mean?"

Joe said, "That's the worst Brooklyn accent I've ever heard."

Joe and Kyle spent the rest of the day discussing the prospect of Joe moving to Texas. The balance of the bourbon slowly disappeared as the day progressed. The following day, Kyle and Joe made their way to the corner diner for breakfast.

With breakfast finished, Kyle announced, "I've got to get back to Texas."

"I appreciate you coming up to see me. If the invitation is still open, I'll be moving to Texas before the end of the year."

Kyle smiled. "We'll have to work on your accent."

Joe acknowledged, "Reckon so." The friends shared a laugh and another cup of coffee.

Chapter 11

TEA TIME

Canyon, Texas

Megan tapped on the front door; Mrs. Milstead opened it and said with a smile, "Megan, you look beautiful."

Megan's pixie-cut hair framed her wrinkle-free face; she wore a straight-cut blue dress with a floral print and black sandals instead of her cowboy boots.

Mrs. Milstead motioned for Megan to enter. "Let's go to the parlor; I've thrown together a tea service."

"Mrs. Milstead, you've never thrown anything together." The women chuckled.

"You can call me Mildred."

"Old habits die hard." Megan handed Mrs. Milstead a pastry box.

Megan followed her hostess down a picture-covered hallway leading to the parlor. She saw pictures of Rowdy in his DEA uniform, her father and Rowdy's father in BDUs holding rifles, her mother and Mrs. Milstead holding a baby, and Megan holding her mother's hand. Mrs. Milstead stood by the parlor door and said, "Those pictures bring back a lot of memories."

"That they do."

"Well, let's open this box and see what treats you've brought." Mrs. Milstead set the box on a square table covered with a rose-colored table cloth; two padded side chairs sat facing each other. A gentle breeze disturbed the lace curtains covering a casement window.

She opened the box. "You've brought my favorite fruit tarts." A tiered service dish sat in the middle of the table; cucumber and salmon finger sandwiches filled two tiers. Mrs. Milstead placed the tarts on the top tier.

She looked at Megan and said, "I'll serve." Mrs. Milstead began pouring the tea.

Megan said, "It seems like yesterday when I'd visit at tea time while little Rowdy had his afternoon nap."

Mrs. Milstead nodded. "Those were happy times. Your dad and my husband were off fighting some war; your mom taught school while I watched you and cared for Rowdy."

"I guess nothing lasts forever."

Mrs. Milstead's tone softened. "The last ten years have not been kind to us."

"I feel like I failed my mother after my father died."

Mrs. Milstead raised her hand. "Nonsense. You took time off from your job to be with her and me when our husbands were killed in action."

"When Mom got sick, I wasn't there to help her."

"You called every day and visited when you could. I was there—remember?"

Megan nodded.

"Let's drink our tea and eat some goodies—shall we?" Mrs. Milstead glanced at the clock and sat upright, saying, "Oh my word. I have to pick up Rowdy. Will you come with me?" Without waiting for an answer, she headed for the door. Megan followed.

Rowdy and the waitress, Janey, were finishing aligning the chairs and setting out coffee cups for the early risers. Mrs. Milstead opened the door. "Are you ready to close up for the day?"

"Yep, let's go."

Janey walked to the door, saying, "See you tomorrow."

Rowdy laughed, "You bet." His mother guided him to the car. Rowdy slid into the passenger seat. He sniffed. "Megan?"

"Yes. How could you tell?"

"You've been wearing the same perfume since you were a teenager. Except for yesterday. I detected horse crap—quite becoming." Rowdy sensed Megan's movement and ducked as her hand grazed his head. "You missed." All shared a laugh.

The three arrived at Mrs. Milstead's home. She asked, "Megan, please stay and help me toss together tonight's meal."

They entered the house. Rowdy excused himself to clean up while the two ladies made their way to the kitchen. Mrs. Milstead walked to the refrigerator and began handing covered dishes to Megan. "All we have to do is heat the food."

Megan stated, "You planned this."

"Yes, dear."

Mrs. Milstead's warm smile always calmed Megan. She asked, "Can I help?"

"I've prepared potato salad and greens. All I have to do is warm up the ham and bake the croissants."

Megan opened the cabinet over the sink. "I'll set the table." The mahogany table and padded chairs sat under a small crystal chandelier.

"How did you know the dishes were there?"

"Same place, different house." She tittered and asked, "Are the place settings in the bottom drawer of the hutch?"

Mrs. Milstead nodded and said, "Let's use the good silverware."

"Top drawer, right side?"

"Yes." Mrs. Milstead began placing already formed croissants on a baking sheet. "All we have to do is wait ten minutes or so."

Rowdy, newly showered, walked into the kitchen. "Are those croissants I smell?"

"Yes."

"Let's eat." Rowdy moved into the dining room and sat.

Megan joined him. Mrs. Milstead set the ham, potato salad, and croissants in the center of the table; salad dishes brimming with fresh produce already sat next to each plate. Megan set the butter dish and individual salt and pepper shakers next to the place settings.

Mrs. Milstead gently grasped Rowdy's hand, reached for Megan's, asked for a blessing on the food, and gave thanks for the three of them being together.

Rowdy asked, "Megan do you remember what you used to call me?"

Megan chuckled. "I had to babysit you when our parents went out. The minute our parents left the house, you ran around the house and taunted me."

Rowdy nodded. "You'd yell, 'Wait till I catch you, you little squirt!'"

"Yes. I called you squirt. When I'd catch you and make you go to bed, you called me string bean or would tell me my chest was a carpenter's dream—flat as a board." Megan smiled. "I remember when I brought home that paratrooper after we eloped. You kicked him in the shins and told him I was your girlfriend."

Rowdy said, "I think I sized him up well."

Megan's face saddened.

Mrs. Milstead stated, "Let's clean up the dishes and have an after-dinner drink."

They stacked the dishes next to the sink. Rowdy adjusted the water temperature and added dish soap. He washed and rinsed each dish and utensil. Megan dried, and Mrs. Milstead put the cleaned dinnerware away.

When all was in good order, Mrs. Milstead said, "Shall we retire to the living room for an aperitif?"

Rowdy and Megan sat in matching wingback chairs facing a light green settee. A gentle breeze filled the room with the smell of cedar from the trees in the front yard. A crystal bowl matched the coasters on the side table next to Rowdy.

Mrs. Milstead placed crystal glasses half-full of Jägermeister next to each of them, along with tall water glasses. "Drink slowly and sip water. This drink is potent."

Rowdy said to Megan, "You never told me what happened with the wildlife department."

"No. And I don't want to talk about it!"

Mrs. Milstead thought, *Megan and Rowdy have wounds they can't talk about yet.* She changed the subject.

"Let's finish our drinks and call it a night."

Chapter 12

A DOOR CLOSES

Brooklyn, New York – November 2015

Joe spent his time getting his house ready to sell. His thoughts were often on the new life he wanted to start in Texas. He knew he was ready to leave New York and suddenly, it all took too much time.

New York real estate prices never dropped during the market crash of 2008. The cost of real estate paused for two months but resumed the rapid price escalation, driving more young people to relocate to Brooklyn. Joe was shocked at the price he received for the house he had inherited from his parents. He knew they had paid twenty thousand dollars for the house when they purchased it. After the real estate sales commission, Joe cleared two hundred and fifty thousand dollars. The new owners needed a month to get ready for the move.

It took the investigators a month to finish reviewing the shooting. A two-line statement printed on page ten of the *New York Post* exonerated the officers involved in the incident. Then, finally, Captain O'Connell called Joe and told him to come to his office. Joe arrived and was greeted by the desk jockeys as a conquering hero.

O'Connell told Joe, "Killing the bank robber was justified, and you can return to duty." Joe looked him in the eye and handed the captain his retirement papers.

O'Connell smiled briefly and said, "Sorry to see you go."

"Right!" Joe turned and walked out of the captain's office.

As Joe exited the precinct, a group of ten patrolmen waited near his car. The men surrounded their old boss. News of Joe's retirement had traveled like wildfire, leaked from the personnel office when he requested his papers, days before the captain called.

Some of the younger officers had tears in their eyes. A senior patrolman handed Joe a carefully wrapped gift. "Everyone except O'Connell contributed." Joe looked at the strange-looking wrapping. "Go ahead and open it."

Joe fumbled as he ripped the paper off a box with the letters Stetson monogrammed across the top. "Well, I'll be!" It was a 200x Stetson Corona cowboy hat.

Joe spent a day visiting the graves of his wife, parents, and son. Then, he continued packing for his move to Texas. The next day, he was surprised by a knock on the door.

Standing on the top step was Willy Simmons. "I've been talking to Kyle. He told me you're moving to West Texas and about your son." Willy ran his hand across his face. "I don't understand why my boy robbed a bank. You could have shot him, but you didn't."

Joe's hands shook, and he said, "I almost did." He crossed his arms and clenched his elbows to stop shaking. "Willy, we killed many people in Mogadishu and Afghanistan, but we went out of our way to save civilians."

He continued, "I interviewed the wounded boy who was with your son. From what I could get out of him, the perp slowly worked his way into Junior's circle of friends. One day, a group of the kids were hanging out drinking beer, bragging about their exploits, and stretching the truth. Hell. That could have been you or me. A bunch of young guys talking themselves into being tough." Joe released the pressure on his forearms. "The perp was from a Mexican cartel and threatened to kill Junior's and his buddy's girlfriends if they didn't help them. The perp was a drug dealer and told the boys he was turning their girls into addicts. If they helped him, he promised to stop selling drugs in their neighborhood."

Willy nodded. "Joe, we've talked about what our lives would have been like if we didn't enlist in the Army." He placed his hand on Joe's shoulder. "We're not supposed to have to bury our children; thanks to you, I won't have to find out what that's like. I can't imagine what you've been living with."

Willy noticed Joe tearing up and embraced his friend. He made Joe promise to come to dinner at his house that night.

That evening, Joe drove to Willy's restored brownstone. As Shirley Simmons answered the door, she said, "Joe, it's been a long time since I've seen you. Come in. Willy's in the living room. Dinner will be ready in a few minutes."

Joe joined his friend in the well-appointed living room. The antique furniture contrasted well with the Victorian design of the house. Willy stood and motioned his friend to a soft-backed chair next to his.

Joe greeted Willy and said, "Shirley has great taste in furniture."

Willy responded, "A lot of people say the same thing. What they question is her choice of husband."

Without cracking a smile, Joe nodded.

"You'll never change." The two men laughed. Willy asked, "Do you still drink that rotgut bourbon?"

"I'll join you to be sociable."

Willy poured two generous glasses of Jim Beam and added a little water and ice cubes. The smell of freshly cooked pot roast complimented the bourbon.

Shirley called out, "Dinner's ready."

Joe and Willy moved to the dining room. Gold-trimmed white porcelain china dinner plates and salad bowls sat on a mahogany table. Four matching chairs were placed around the table. The placemats were embroidered lace; silver utensils bracketed the setting. A Murano blown glass chandelier hung from the ceiling, casting a colorful glow. Joe smiled and said, "This is too elegant for a burnt-out cop."

Shirley motioned Joe to sit at the head of the table. Her gentle hand grasped Willy's and Joe's hands. "Lord, we ask your blessing. Wrap your arms around us and help us to get through these trying times." Her delicate hands belied their strength as she ended the prayer.

The men stared down at their hands.

Shirley whispered, "Let's eat and talk about the future."

The men talked about Joe's son and Willy Jr. When the men paused, Shirley spoke. "You both have reached the end of your civil service careers. Willy just put in his papers to retire from the fire department."

Willy explained, "I've been a fireman for twenty years and a lieutenant for five of those years. I've got enough time plus my five years of military service to guarantee me a decent retirement. I think we can supplement our retirement if Shirley takes in laundry." They all laughed.

Shirley waved that idea away and remarked, "I did the cooking. You two can do the dishes."

Joe said, "I bet you could qualify for a disability pension from the Veterans Administration."

Shirley glanced at her husband. "Why would you qualify for disability?"

Joe fumbled his words. "I suffer from foot in mouth disease."

Willy shook his head, laughing. "Same old Joe." He glanced at Shirley. "We'll talk later."

The trio cleared the table, and Willy washed the dishes. He tossed the drying cloth to Joe. "Do the honors." Shirley's smile relaxed the two men.

As they worked, Joe outlined a course of action for getting their son a minimum sentence and maybe an innocent verdict. Joe handed the dried dishes to Shirley and said, "I was the arresting officer. If the DA doesn't call me as a witness, I'd be surprised." He looked at Willy. "Have you hired an attorney for your son?"

"Yes." He gave Joe the attorney's name.

Joe said, "I know him. I'll see him before I leave town. Has there been a bail hearing?"

"No."

Joe's brow wrinkled. "You've got to get that boy out of Riker's ASAP. He's only a kid." He continued, "Your son was into something he couldn't handle. The dead robber had a cartel tattoo."

The men talked more about the legal defense strategy. Joe told his friend he would use his connections in the correctional institution to see that Willy Jr. was isolated from the hardened criminals and arrange for a bail hearing.

Joe looked up at Willy. "We'll get through this."

Willy and Shirley walked Joe to the door. Shirley was overcome with emotion and pulled Joe to her and cried, "How can we thank you?"

Joe held his friend's wife at arm's length. "Ask Willy why I'm still alive." He kissed her forehead and walked out into the night.

Chapter 13

LEAVING BROOKLYN, NEW YORK

Joe packed his clothes, awards, and picture albums in the back seat of his new Ford F-150. The salesman said it was just like the Texas Edition. His gun repair equipment was packed in their original boxes and secured in the bed of the truck. He'd arranged with his bank to transfer ten thousand dollars to the Happy State Bank in Canyon. He planned to maintain his account with his investment banker. He hadn't looked at his statement in a long time and was surprised when he pulled up his Schwab account and saw his balance was up to seven figures.

He liked the smell of newness and all the modern gadgets in the truck. He thought to himself, *I hope this GPS works.* He entered the directions to Canyon, Texas, then called Kyle to say, "I'm on my way."

"Do you know how to get here?"

"No, but my brand-new GPS does. It says 1,725 miles. Two long days and I'll be there."

"We'll keep the light on for you. If you get lost, call me."

"That'll be the day."

"By God, you already sound like a Texan."

Joe used his best Brooklyn accent. "See yuz guys latuh." He chuckled and disconnected the call.

Joe enjoyed driving, but not in New York City. He left Brooklyn at 5 a.m. and drove across the Verrazano Bridge before the commuters were on the road. By 7 a.m., Joe was approaching the Delaware Water Gap. He stopped to admire the scenery.

His thoughts wandered to the last time he'd passed this point. It was just before his son went to boot camp. They planned a father-son hunting trip and spent time cleaning their rifles and inspecting camping equipment. When Joe had mentioned to a friend they would camp out in tents in the winter, the friend thought they were crazy. The truth was Joe and his son enjoyed winter camping as long as the temperature didn't drop below zero. They saw numerous animals they could shoot, lining them up in their sights and yelling "bang." The weather cooperated and they enjoyed the solitude.

Joe reminisced about his life with Anna. They had enjoyed the same music. Over the years, he had loaded their favorite songs on his iPod. Their music taste varied from reggae to classical. It brought a smile to his face, remembering his son's feigned horror when he turned on his music. His new

F-150 had a Bluetooth interface compatible with his iPod. After two tries, the connection worked. Joe put the truck in drive and hit play. He laughed at the first song, "Amarillo by Morning," by George Strait. To this song, he and Anna used to practice the two-step. She would say with a smile, "You learned half the dance."

As Ravel's "Bolero" ended, he pulled off the interstate on the south side of Indianapolis and thought, *It might take two and a half days to make the trip.* A Holiday Inn Express was just off the highway, and after he checked in, he headed for the Cracker Barrel restaurant next to the hotel. After he was seated and had ordered his food, he dialed Kyle.

His friend answered. "You should have left sooner. Dove season started two days ago."

"I should be there the day after tomorrow."

"That GPS won't get you to the house. Call me when you get off the interstate."

"Will do." He ended the call.

While he was waiting for his food, he tried to solve the Triangle Peg puzzle. After three tries, his score was at sub-moron. The young waiter brought his food, and Joe asked, "Can you solve this thing?"

"Sure, I'll show you." In less than a minute, a solitary peg remained. "Will there be anything else?"

Bewildered, Joe answered, "No, thank you." *I better leave a good tip.*

The next evening, he was west of Oklahoma City, driving into a setting sun. Joe thought, *It's time to get some shut-eye.*

He found another Holiday Inn Express with rooms available. The desk clerk was cheerful and welcoming. She spent time explaining the breakfast schedule and asked if he needed any directions. He thought, *What a different attitude from the Northeast.* The television sat idle as he relaxed in the hotel room and thought about his new life.

Chapter 14

THE EARLY YEARS

The next morning, the road stretched, seemingly endlessly, in front of Joe and his thoughts drifted again to the past. It felt like a chapter of his life was closing behind him, while new opportunities opened before him.

Joe's memory of his grandfather making wine in the cellar always brought a smile to his face. His grandfather tended his grapevines like a protective parent. He taught Joe how to press grapes and make wine. As the wine fermented, he told his grandson to press his ear against the barrel. He'd ask, "Do you hear the wine talking to you?"

"Yes, Grandpa. When will the wine be ready?"

"I listen every day. The wine will tell us when it's ready."

One day his grandpa said, "Maybe the wine is ready."

The smell of fermented grapes filled the cellar. The older man poured the first glass, took a sip, and handed it to him. The new wine tasted bitter. Joe smiled and said, "It's good."

His grandpa laughed. "This wine has to age for another year."

He handed Joe another sample of wine from a dust-covered barrel.

"Grandpa, you're right. The new wine has to grow up." His grandfather patted his head.

One day a barrel rolled on Grandpa's foot. He let loose a jumble of Italian expletives.

His grandmother heard the words and shouted, "Shut your mouth."

Grandpa yelled, "Yes, Mama." He winked at Joe.

Joe's father worked for the sanitation department. He'd worked his way up from garbage collector to area commander. He dressed in a suit to go to work. He'd change into his sanitation department uniform at work; the neighbors never knew what he did for a living.

Joe's father loved hunting. Each year he'd go deer hunting in upstate New York. Their neighbors would surround his car when he brought home a deer tied across the car's front fender. The dead deer would be tied up in the basement and allowed to age. Then, when his father thought it was ready, he'd remove the skin and slice it into portions. It was a treat when his mother cooked deer meat. Joe was ten years old when he accompanied his father on his first hunting trip, learning how to stalk and handle a gun safely in the field. The first time Joe handled a rifle, he was 12 years old.

During the year, his father cleaned and repaired his rifles. Many people brought their firearms in need of repair to his father. By the age of 14, Joe could disassemble a variety of weapons. He didn't know it, but he was developing skills that would save his life.

Chapter 15

SCHOOL IN BROOKLYN— THE EARLY YEARS

Joe went to the local grammar school on Gates Avenue in Brooklyn, P.S. 26. It was a large red granite building. To a youngster from a four-story tenement, the school appeared enormous. The area was racially mixed. The differences in ethnicity were meaningless to young children, but this all changed in junior high school. Groups formed by race; it didn't make sense to Joe. Joe usually walked to and from school with his cousins. One day he was kept after school and had to walk home alone. The schoolyard was a large quadrangle where students played stickball. Not to interfere with the game in progress, he walked down the fence line. Without warning, a group of black teenagers surrounded him and pelted him with rocks. Willy Simmons ran to his side. "Y'all leave him alone." At 12 years old, Willy stood six feet tall and weighed nearly two hundred pounds—no one messed with Willy. The gang disbursed. Willy walked Joe home, and a lasting friendship began.

When Joe graduated from P.S. 26, his family moved to the Bensonhurst section of Brooklyn, a predominately Italian neighborhood. Joe applied to Brooklyn Technical High. Willy was accepted in Boys High, in another part of Brooklyn. The two boys vowed that their friendship would never end. They spent time together whenever they could.

During his senior year, a visit to an Army recruiter changed Joe's life. He took the Armed Services Vocational Aptitude Battery (ASVAB) tests.

An excited Joe called his friend. "Hey Willy, guess what I've just taken? The Aptitude Test for the Army."

"Me too!"

"Well, I'll be. Maybe we can serve together?"

Willy chuckled, "I guess I'll have to keep the big kids from picking on you."

When they received their test results, they made an appointment with the recruiter.

A bulldog-faced sergeant met them. "You two want to serve together?"

In unison, they answered, "Yes, sir."

"I don't know how you managed this, but you're both in the 90th percentile."

Willy frowned. "I don't know what that means."

The sergeant explained, "After boot camp, if you complete it with high enough scores, you'll be allowed to attend jump school, and if you pass jump school with high enough performance ratings, you'll be eligible for Ranger school."

Joe smiled. "Put that in writing, and we'll sign up." Willy nodded his agreement.

"You two are pretty sure of yourselves."

"Yes, sir." They answered in unison.

Chapter 16

A DOOR OPENS

Canyon, Texas

The GPS didn't fail Joe until he exited I-27 in Canyon. A pleasant female voice informed him that "directions to your destination are not available." *Time to call Kyle.*

"I'm at the Canyon exit, and the GPS can't give me instructions to your house."

"That's good. Take State Highway 217 five miles, turn south on to South Osage St., and drive two miles; I'm the only house on the road."

"Which way is south?"

"Left. Use your compass."

"Okay, see you in a few minutes."

Kyle chuckled. "If you don't get lost."

Joe stopped in front of a two-story wood and brick house with an extended porch. The front door opened and Kyle burst through the door.

"Joe, how are you? Come in. My wife is waiting to meet you."

The columned entrance led to a foyer; matching tiles formed a diamond pattern. Standing at the door was a slim woman with silver and gold hair and a warm smile. She extended her hand.

"My name is Britta. I feel like I've known you forever." She pulled him toward her and hugged him. "We're just about to eat. You must be hungry." She tilted her head. "There's the washroom," and pointed to a door. "Wash up and join us in the dining room."

Kyle commented, "Do what she says." He smiled and winked.

The dining room's pine table adorned with bone china and plain silverware awaited the guests. A glass of ice water and a generous salad sat at each place setting.

Britta spoke, "Y'all eat your salad while I get the chicken and vegetables cooked. If you want a beer, Kyle will get it." She headed for the kitchen.

Joe smiled. "She's a real beauty and full of spirit."

"She's like having a good bay horse. You can work her all week, clean her up, and take her to town on Saturday."

From the kitchen Britta called, "I heard that."

Joe was tired from the long trip. That night, the bed felt good and he slept until 9 a.m. He showered, dressed, and headed downstairs. Kyle and Britta sat in the kitchen drinking coffee. Kyle commented, "Glad you made it down. It's almost time for lunch."

Britta said, "Don't listen to him. How do scrambled eggs, bacon, and toast sound?"

"Perfect." Joe made his way to the coffee pot and filled a cup. Britta prepared his breakfast and placed the plate in front of Joe.

"Thank you." He smiled at her.

After Joe finished his second cup of coffee, Kyle asked, "Would you like to take a ride with me? I have to check cattle."

"Let's do it."

They jumped into Kyle's ranch truck, a dark blue 1997 F-250 diesel, with the name K.B. Ranch on the doors. Kyle had removed the original cargo bed and added a flatbed; a trailer hitching ball occupied the bed's center, and a toolbox was mounted behind the rear window. Stacks of feed secured with a strap took up most of the bed's space.

Joe commented, "This truck is almost a classic."

"It is a classic, I reckon. It's the best diesel Ford ever made. It only has two hundred thousand miles on it—barely broke in." Kyle inserted the key in the ignition and waited 30 seconds, and turned the key. The engine roared to life. "A little noisy; you'll get used to it." They headed south on a dirt road. A plume of dust followed the truck.

After two miles, Joe asked, "When do we get to your land?"

"The land on your side of the road is all mine. It runs to Palo Duro Canyon. We've shifted the cows to their winter pasture." The road ended at a cattle guard with round pipes embedded in the road, and a barbed-wire gate.

Kyle explained, "The gate probably isn't necessary. The cows won't walk on pipes. But better safe than sorry."

Joe got out of the truck to open the gate. After a battle, the wire that secured the entrance to a thick cedar post gave way. Joe hauled the gate to one side. Kyle joined Joe in his struggle to attach the top wire.

Kyle commented, "Jose built this gate. He forgets that normal humans have to open them." A cedar-lined path cascaded down the canyon wall. The trail dropped out of sight.

"This is something else." Joe peered over the dashboard and asked, "How do we get down to the bottom?"

"Old Blue knows the way." Kyle laughed and guided the truck down the trail. Joe gripped the dashboard and dug in his feet. Kyle smiled. "Don't worry. I haven't lost anyone yet." The truck inched down the canyon wall. Every two hundred feet, a dirt terrace broke up the nearly vertical descent. Finally, the trail ended at another gate. Kyle was about to get out of the truck.

Joe said, "I'll get it." He opened and closed the gate and climbed back into the truck. "How much land do you own?"

"I lease this place. The family that owns it knew my father. They don't run any cattle and don't want to sell the land. I have grazing rights. A bunch of Dallas lawyers has hunting rights." The road wound around mesquite bushes and cedar trees. They crossed a dry riverbed.

Kyle remarked, "You should see this river after a big rain. It's something else." They drove to a windmill that fed a water tank. About 50 cows stood or rested near the tank. Kyle honked the truck horn, and the cows walked toward the truck. "Give me a hand. Open one of the feed sacks and spread the cubes along the road behind the truck. I'll take another one and spread it on the other side of the road."

"Those cows are running at us!"

"Don't worry; they don't eat meat."

"Very funny."

There were three more water tanks to visit. After the last stop, they came to a barbed-wire fence stretched across the valley. Kyle announced, "Time for lunch."

Joe remarked, "I didn't think we'd stop until we reached New York."

Kyle smiled and asked, "Do you want a bologna sandwich?"

"Sounds good." They sat on the truck bed to eat.

"Well, Joe, what's your plan?"

"I like your idea. I want to open a rifle and pistol repair shop in town."

Kyle nodded, saying, "I already know at least a dozen customers."

The drive back was uneventful. Joe relaxed and enjoyed the ride. As they crossed a streambed, a family of wild hogs ran across the road. Kyle slammed on the brakes, grabbed a rifle from the rack behind the seat, and jumped out of the truck; three shots echoed through the valley. One large boar collapsed. Two massive hogs and about ten piglets scampered to safety.

Joe laughed. "Next time, give me the rifle."

"That'll be the day! These wild hogs are getting out of hand. They breed two or three times a year and have between five and ten piglets each time. It doesn't take long for a bunch of hogs to destroy a pasture."

After ensuring that the hog was dead, the partners drove back up the canyon trail. Joe asked, "Are you going to load the dead hog?"

"Nah, I've got half a freezer full of sausage."

"You're just going to leave it."

"Yep, the coyotes will eat it."

A few minutes later, Joe asked, "What type of bushes are these?"

"The bright green ones are mesquites, and the spiny furry ones are cedars."

Kyle stopped. Joe stepped out of the truck to look at the bushes. "These mesquites have ugly-looking thorns."

"That's why we wear chaps."

"The cedars smell like pines."

"Wait until the winter when they molt and spray their pollen. It's something to see."

The men arrived home near 5 p.m. Britta greeted them with a smile. "Y'all wash up and drink a beer. Dinner will be ready in an hour."

Kyle said, "Yes, dear. Maybe we'll have two."

She responded, "That's your limit."

"Yes, dear."

Chapter 17

MEETING RACHEL

Britta looked at Joe during dinner. "Kyle tells me you're thinking of opening a rifle repair business?"

"Correct. My dad and grandpa taught me. I've had my gunsmith license in New York for years. I checked with the State of Texas and applied for a Texas gunsmith license. I sent them a copy of my federal license, and they issued me a Texas license."

"You and Kyle are alike. He's always reminding me to plan."

Kyle smiled. "If you fail to plan, you're planning to fail."

With a smile, Britta covered her ears and then asked, "Joe, what's your plan?"

"Tomorrow, I think I'll go to Canyon and see what storefronts are for rent."

She answered, "My cousin Rachel is a part-time real estate agent. Maybe she can help."

At breakfast the following day, Britta called her cousin. "Rachel, I'm sending a friend of Kyle's to see you. He's looking for a place to rent for a new gun repair shop."

The conversation consisted of "Yup," "Okay," and a closing comment, "He's a Yankee, but he's a friend of Kyle's from the Army. Love you. See you at church."

She turned toward Joe. "Here's one of Rachel's cards. She's expecting you."

Joe asked, "Where should I meet her?"

"I'll give you directions."

They stacked the breakfast dishes. Kyle headed for the door, saying, "I have to meet one of the ranch hands at the north pasture. We have some fence to fix."

Britta smiled at Joe. "You and Rachel will get along fine."

The drive to Canyon took ten minutes. Joe arrived at Rachel's store just before 8 a.m. The sign on the window said, "Pottery & More," and "Rachel Meadows, Licensed Realtor" on the lower right-hand corner. Joe parked and stepped out of his truck. An attractive, slim woman exited the vehicle parked next to him. Gray streaks in her red hair framed her oval face.

"Y'all must be Joe D'Angelo. Rachel Meadows, pleased to meet you." Her handshake was firm; a warm smile and light gray eyes put Joe at ease. "Come in."

She opened the door and ushered Joe inside. Her office in the rear of the store had a high-backed chair and a side chair. "Have a seat." She began, "How was your trip from New York City?"

"Long."

Rachel laughed, "You answer just like Kyle. Britta told me about you. We're happy you moved to Texas. If I remember right, you're a retired New York City police officer. You and Kyle served in the Army together, and you're interested in opening a gun repair shop."

"Correct."

Chapter 18

EVERYONE KNOWS JOE

Rachel and Joe spent the morning discussing Joe's plans for a gun repair shop. As they talked, an older woman entered the store.

The woman smiled at Joe.

"You're Kyle's friend from New York." Then, without waiting for a response, she asked, "What church do you go to?"

Joe fumbled for an answer. Her blue eyes twinkled.

She didn't wait for his answer. "Please come to our church, the First United Methodist Church; it's on Fourth Avenue."

Rachel interrupted, "Aunt May, give the man a chance to get settled."

Aunt May responded, "I want to invite him to our church before those Baptists do."

Rachel chuckled. "Okay."

The old lady's face brightened as she looked at Joe. "Y'all come visit." As she opened the door to leave, she called out. "Honey, save that new pot with the rose painted on it for me."

"Yes, ma'am."

It was approaching 10 a.m. Rachel announced, "Time for coffee. Join me?"

"Sure, why not?"

As they left the store, Rachel hung a sign on a plastic clip that read, *Be back at 10:30.* They walked a few blocks to the Juan's place, their usual morning hangout.

Rachel asked, "You're not a Starbucks person, are you?"

"No."

"Good."

Juan's Restaurant and Coffee Shop sat on the corner of Fifteenth Street and Fifth Avenue.

As they entered, the smell of marinated steak greeted him. At the back of the store sat a woodburning stove vented through the ceiling. A rotund Hispanic man scrutinized the meat. Then he noticed the new customers. "Rachel, is that Kyle's Yankee friend?"

"Yup."

The man met Rachel and Joe as they reached a table where three other men sat. He wiped his hand on an apron that had seen better days.

"Juan Herrera. Nice to meet you."

"Likewise."

"Y'all sure talk funny."

Joe put on his best Brooklyn accent. "Did you have a relative that played for the Houston Astros?"

The three men at the table stood. A tall redheaded, broad-shouldered man laughed, "He got you, Juan!"

Juan smiled. "I'll bring two coffees. Most Yankees like cream and sugar, yes?"

Joe responded, "A shot of tequila suits me fine."

As the group sat and Juan fetched two cups of coffee, Rachel made the introductions. The redhead, J.C. Sparks, nodded. The next member of the coffee crew was Troy Hammond; his buzz-cut brown and silver hair went with his military bearing. Ralph Emory was a short man, maybe five foot six. His left shoulder drooped, and his withered arm hung from his shoulder.

The conversation centered on Joe's moving to Texas. Troy commented, "Well, another Yankee."

Rachel's eyes flashed. "You're an Okie from Muskogee, and we welcomed you."

Troy was red-faced. "Just kidding."

The group listened as Joe explained how he wanted to open a gunsmith shop. Sparks said, "My .30-30 is starting to drift." He asked, "What do you think?"

"The sight probably needs to be realigned, and it wouldn't hurt to take it apart and oil the parts."

"I don't think I've ever taken that rifle apart. When are you going to open?"

Rachel answered, "We've been working on finding him a store to rent."

As if on cue, the group stood and said their goodbyes.

Ralph looked at Joe. "Y'all come back."

As Joe and Rachel walked back to her office, Joe said, "Everyone seems to know everything about me."

Rachel looked shocked. "Of course. Now let's find you an empty store."

He scratched his head. *Don't these people have better things to talk about?*

Rachel stopped. "I've been thinking." She walked to the empty store next to hers. "I own this store and the two next to it. Maybe one of them will suit your needs." Her cell phone buzzed, and Rachel looked at the caller's name. "I have to take this call. Here are the keys. Why don't you look around? When you finish, let's talk."

Chapter 19

OLD FRIENDS

Rachel pressed talk. She recognized the number. "Sue, how are you?" She listened for a minute and dashed into her store. "Slow down."

Susan Reed was a longtime friend and college roommate. They met at the University of California when they were both in the School of the Arts and Architecture. Sue majored in painting, and Rachel studied pottery.

Rachel was from a ranching family, and Sue spent her summers at her uncle's ranch in Wyoming. The friends split their vacations between Texas and Wyoming.

"Tomorrow, you'll probably read that Harold has committed fraud and is in jail." Her husband, Harold Boeddeker, was an investment banker with a major brokerage firm. After their marriage, Sue continued her art career using her family name.

The two friends made it a practice to talk monthly. Rachel had known Sue's marriage wasn't going well; Sue never mentioned it. The last time they were together was when Rachel's husband had died in a farming accident, years ago.

Rachel asked, "Are you okay?"

"No."

"I think we need to talk. But unfortunately, this conversation won't be a short one."

"I'm going to pack up and head your way tomorrow."

"Do you want me to fly out and drive with you?"

"I'll be alright. I just need my best friend to talk to."

Sue took three days to get ready for the trip. Rachel called her after the second day.

"I haven't heard from you. How are things going?"

"I'm okay. There are several things I have to take care of before I leave." She paused. "I want to bring my two horses. I'll need a place to board them."

"Not a problem. I board my horses at Kyle Mitchell's place. Are you going to drive straight through?"

"No. I'll overnight at Benson, Arizona, with Emma and Clint Bigham."

"Tell them I said hi and call me when you leave Benson."

"Will do."

The drive from San Diego to Benson seemed longer to Sue than it was. The highway from Yuma to Tucson felt like the journey's longest stretch, although it wasn't. The monotonous scenery through the Sonoran Desert was hot and dry. Gray sand stretched to bare, lifeless mountains in the distance; saguaro cactus provided the only distraction. The outside temperature registered 95 degrees, hotter than usual for this time of the year. The truck's air conditioning was overwhelmed and threatened to overheat the vehicle; the only option was to turn it off and open windows. The blast of hot air leached the water from her body. The desert landscape summed up her feelings—lonely and empty.

Finally, she arrived in Benson with no mishaps. The owner of the ranch, Clint Bigham, was waiting as she pulled in. As she opened her truck's door, he asked, "How are you?" He was never at a loss for words. "It's been a long time since I've seen you. Dinner's ready, but let's get your horses settled first. Emma has set a plate for you."

As Clint removed his dust-encrusted cowboy hat, his weathered hands embraced Sue's. "I thought maybe your friend from Canyon would come with you?"

"Nope, that's where I'm going."

It was hard to be in a bad mood around Clint, and Sue smiled. "Let's get the horses settled. I'm anxious to see Emma."

"Well, you know, she hasn't changed. Still mean as a rattlesnake."

From the porch, looking at her husband, Emma commented. "You put her horses up. We'll be in the kitchen." Her deliberate steps gave away her age. Her strong arms embraced Sue. "Come in." Over her shoulder, she yelled, "Get moving, Clint, or I'll throw your dinner to the hogs."

Clint set his Stetson hat on his balding head. "I told you she's just the same."

Sue chuckled. "You two will never change." She'd known them for nearly 30 years. Clint and Emma were breeders and trainers of horses. Sue had bought her two horses from them several years ago.

After dinner, the Bigham's washed and dried the dishes while Sue sat at the kitchen table. Clint smiled. "I wish you'd stay awhile. The horses need work."

Sue looked down at her hands.

Emma asked, "What's wrong?"

Sue's lip quivered, and a tear rolled down her cheek. "I'm divorcing my husband and moving to Texas." Clint and Emma sat with her at the table and spent the evening talking about Sue's husband's arrest for fraud and his infidelity.

The following day after breakfast, Clint went out and closed the latches on the trailer and checked the brake lights hookup. Then the Bighams helped Sue load the horses.

As she was ready to go, Clint held Sue's hands and said, "Take some time before you get back in the saddle."

"I know the horses need work," she said.

Emma embraced her and whispered, "He wasn't talking about the horses."

Chapter 20

A NEW HOME

From Benson, Arizona, to Canyon, Texas

Sue pulled onto the road from the Bigham place and drove to the on-ramp of Interstate 10. As she headed up the highway entrance, a sliver of yellow punctured the early-morning gray. The bleak desert landscape gradually changed. Cactus gave way to cedar trees; cattle grazed on sparse stands of grass. Interstate 10 rose and fell with the landscape. Passing by the Rex Allen Museum brought a smile as she remembered stopping there with Rachel. Allen, known as the "Singing Cowboy," was born in Wilcox, Arizona. A museum honoring their native son displayed the film star's memorabilia.

At Las Cruces, New Mexico, she headed north on Route 70 and climbed into the San Augustin Mountains. As the road descended the mountain, White Sands National Park glistened in the afternoon sun. She put on sunglasses to reduce the glare.

Sue planned to stop in Mescalero, New Mexico, the headquarters of the Apache Nation, at the tribal gas station because no federal taxes added to the price of gasoline. She retrieved two water buckets from the horse trailer, opened the screened window, and tried to hoist the bucket to the clip above the window. She wanted the horses to have one more drink before the final leg of the nine-hour journey. A young man with twin braids smiled and assisted her with the heavy bucket and again with the second one.

She tried to hand the young man a five-dollar bill.

He tipped his hat. "That's not necessary, ma'am."

With the gas tanks filled and the horses tended to, she went into the Mescalero store. The store was a riot of colorful headdresses and beaded garments. They also had a snack stand and a coffee pot. With her purchases in hand, she found a bench in front of the store. It was a bright shiny day; the tree-covered Sierra Blanca Mountains surrounded the town. The anxiety that filled her with dread when she left San Diego evaporated.

The drive through Ruidoso should be quick, she thought. A sign advertised the new Kenneth Wyatt Art Gallery. She whispered, "I've got to stop." Sue was familiar with Wyatt's art and thought he had only one gallery, in Tulia, Texas.

The lady in the gallery greeted her. "May I help you?"

"I'm just passing through and I noticed the billboard. I'm familiar with Mr. Wyatt's work."

"What's your name?"

"Susan Reed. I'm from California."

"Oh, my God. Mr. Wyatt talks about you. You're a famous abstract artist."

Sue blushed. "Not really, but I appreciate the compliment."

The gallery manager and Sue spent several minutes talking about art. Finally, she asked Sue, "What brings you east?"

"I'm relocating to Canyon, Texas."

"I'll tell Kenneth about our visit. You must stop in Tulia and see him." The manager offered Sue a to-go cup of coffee.

As she drove, she sipped her coffee and thought, *Next stop, Canyon. Then what?*

Chapter 21

RACHEL'S HOUSE

Canyon, Texas

Sue thought, *Better call Rachel.* She pulled over outside Ruidoso Downs.

"Hi, Rachel."

"Where are you?"

"Just leaving Ruidoso."

"That's great. You'll be here in about four hours. It'll still be daylight. Come to my house, and we'll get your horses settled."

The bright sunlight above her as she rode through the green mountains brought a smile to her face. *This country is so beautiful.*

Traffic was light, and the occasional white cumulus clouds promised good weather. Once out of the mountains, the road first rolled through low hills then straightened out. Roswell, New Mexico, broke up the desert landscape. Her smile widened as she drove by the posters proclaiming the town as the home of the alien spacecraft that landed in 1947. Sue chuckled and thought of the propeller heads walking around campus talking about Area 51. Next was Clovis, New Mexico, and then Canyon.

Rachel's house was located two miles from State Highway 217, east of the city of Canyon. The single-story house sat two hundred feet off a dirt road. A base of light-colored caliche covered the dirt road and driveway to the house. An overhang provided shade from the summer sun and winter snow.

Sue had visited Rachel several times. The last time was for the funeral of Rachel's husband. She parked on the ranch road next to Rachel's sprawling house. Her friend came out of her house and walked across the manicured lawn. The friends embraced. "You look tired. I'll drive your rig to the barn and unload your horses."

"Let's do it together," Sue said as she unlocked the trailer door and slid back the partition that kept the horses in an oblique position during the ride. She untied the lead rope and followed the horse as it backed out of the confinement; Rachel held the lead line. Sue backed up the other horse and guided it out.

Rachel remarked, "The horses made the trip well."

"Clint and Emma gave them some alfalfa, and I watered them in Mescalero, New Mexico."

Rachel motioned Sue to follow her. It was light enough to see the paddocks, which looked different than Sue remembered. Instead of one large pasture, fencing separated the area into several paddocks. Rachel opened a gate and walked her horse in; Sue followed. They removed the horse's headstall. Sue patted her horse as it moved toward the feed and water.

"Well, there's water and feed. The horses can sniff each other across the fence."

Sue smiled. "All I need for now is my overnight bag. I don't want to fool with the other stuff."

"Okay, grab it and let's go in. We've got a lot of talking to do."

Sue thought, *Rachel's way of expressing herself never ceases to amaze me.*

Inside, the entrance hallway ran down the middle of the house to an oversized, open kitchen and family room. The master suite occupied a private area off the family room—three bedrooms with private baths and an office flanked the hallway. Western art and two of Sue's impressionist paintings hung on the walls. Clay pottery sat in the open spaces.

A glass of water and a sandwich kept Sue from nodding off. Rachel walked her friend to her room and said goodnight. Sue thought sadly, *Rachel and her husband had planned to have a large family.* A good night's sleep would help cure her melancholy.

The following day, Sue joined Rachel in the breakfast nook at the back of the kitchen. The windows captured the rising sun. Rachel smiled as Sue poured a cup of coffee and joined her.

Rachel began the conversation. "Do you want to talk about your divorce?"

Sue wrinkled her brow. "There's not much to talk about; Harold's in jail; he needs a bond of ten million dollars before he can be released. " Sue sipped her coffee. "I don't know if I mentioned it, but we had separate tax returns and checking accounts. I painted using my maiden name. Harold didn't want the pittance I earned to complicate his tax return."

She set down the coffee cup. "At gatherings with his business friends, he joked about his starving artist wife."

Rachel added, "I'm no lawyer, but if you didn't sign any of Harold's contracts or loan agreements, your assets should be protected."

"That's what my attorney told me. My artwork, truck, car, horses, and trailer are all in my name." Sue paused. "A driver is going to deliver my car sometime this week. He'll call when he gets to Canyon."

"When do you think Harold's trial will be?"

"From what my attorney and I can figure out, it's going to be a long, complex trial. Several of his partners are also in jail, awaiting trial. So when I told my attorney about my plan to move here, he thought it was a good idea that I should have my checking account and investment accounts transferred."

Rachel nodded and stood. "Let's make breakfast and go tend to the horses."

Sue's face lit up. "Just like our college days."

"I have to open my store at nine. Do you want to come to town with me? I have a plan I'd like to discuss with you."

"I need to sort out the stuff I packed in the living section of the trailer; if it's okay with you, I want to work out my horses in your round pen."

"I understand. You know where the food is; help yourself."

"I'll prepare dinner tonight. Any requests?"

"No mac and cheese!" Rachel added, "We lived on that stuff for four years in college. Tilt your head; I bet one of your eyes is still yellow." The friends shared a laugh.

Chapter 22

THE GUNSMITH STORE

Canyon, Texas

Rachel pulled into her parking spot. She noticed a truck parked in front of her store. *Oh Lord, I forgot that I rented that place to Kyle's friend.* She looked at her watch—8:45. *What was his name?* She walked into the empty store.

Joe spotted her. "I'm glad you stopped by. I need to talk to you about my plan to remodel the place."

She glanced at her watch; it finally struck her; his name was Joe. "Sure, Joe. I have a few minutes—what did you have in mind?"

Joe explained that a new customer counter would serve as a workbench and restrict customer access to his living quarters. The twenty-foot entrance area ended with a plasterboard wall. A plywood door opened into a kitchen area, adjoining space, and a living/dining room. The bedroom area was an enclosed space at the far end of the building. A twenty-foot hallway led to the rear door; halfway down the hall, a door opened into the sleeping area.

Rachel commented, "You've got this well planned out."

Joe replied, "This must have been a small shop with the owner living in the rear."

"Yes, it was an insurance agency; Ralph Emory got his start here."

Rachel answered Joe's quizzical expression. "You met him at the coffee shop the other day."

"Oh yes, I remember him."

Before Joe could continue, Rachel added, "He got his shriveled left arm when he was wounded in Iraq."

Joe's face flushed. "I'm sorry."

"You'll get to know Ralph; he's a good guy."

Joe continued, "If my plan is okay with you, I'd like to get started as soon as possible."

A delivery man entered and called out, "Mr. D'Angelo, I have the wood and supplies you ordered." He spied Rachel and asked, "Is this the retired New York Cop?"

She smiled and said, "Yes."

Joe asked, "Can you bring the delivery to the back door?"

"Not a problem."

Joe led Rachel to the back door. "Does everyone in town know my life story?"

"Yep."

Joe helped the delivery man unload his purchases. He glanced at Rachel. "I've got a lot of work to do."

Rachel took the hint and stated, "I'm only two doors down if you need anything."

"Thank you." Joe turned his back and began inventorying his supplies.

Rachel opened the door to her store and thought, *He's a strange duck.*

Her Aunt May stopped by to make sure Rachel hadn't sold the pottery piece with a rose on it yet. A discussion followed about where Aunt May would put the piece in her home.

Rachel smiled, saying, "If you add one more thing in your house, it'll explode."

"I'll think of a place to put it. Now, don't sell it."

"No, ma am."

"Bless your heart." Aunt May waved and stepped out the door.

A real estate client stopped by to discuss a problem with the title to his land. They agreed on how to correct the issue. By then it was approaching 10 a.m. Time for coffee.

Rachel opened the door to the new gunsmith store and saw that Joe was assembling his workbench and had partially painted the store. She stated, "That's a nice color."

Joe commented, "Light blue is a good color for a gun store. Bold colors bring out aggression."

She smiled, "Did you study the psychology of colors?"

"Yes, I did, at the police academy."

Rachel smiled and motioned for Joe to follow her. "It's time for a coffee break."

"I have to take a pass. Too much work to do. But thanks for the invite." But he thought, *I've got to loosen up; she's being neighborly.*

That night at dinner, Kyle asked, "How did your day go?"

Joe answered, "I've started getting my shop and apartment squared away."

"There's no hurry to move out; we're enjoying your company."

Britta added, "I've enjoyed hearing y'all talk about your time in the Army."

Joe smiled and said, "I appreciate all you've done for me, but I'm anxious to start my new career."

Kyle spoke, "I was hoping you'd tag along when we round up the cattle."

"That sounds like fun. Only one question: which end of the horse do you get on?"

"Maybe you need a few lessons."

Chapter 23

THE WINDOW PAINTER

Joe finished laying out the designs for his renovations and painted the walls in his new store. Next, he hired a glazier to replace the front window with bulletproof glass. Then Joe thought, *I need a window sign.*

He remembered seeing a store on the square that advertised sign paintings and works of art. *Let's see if the artist can design a window display.*

A man approached as Joe entered the store. "Howdy, my name is Brad Cox. How can I help you?"

"I'm Joe D'Angelo. I'm opening a gunsmith store next to Rachel's gift store. I need a window sign."

Brad sat at his work table and motioned Joe to sit on a stool by his side. "Hum, let's think on this." Brad opened a sketch pad and began drawing. He asked Joe, "Are you going to sell guns?"

"Nope, just repair them."

Brad's pencil moved effortlessly across a page in his sketch pad. Joe was amazed at how the window design took shape. A crouching hunter pointed a rifle at a distant deer bounding over a log. Transparent clouds filled the sky. Between the hunting scene and the clouds, Brad wrote a banner in calligraphy: "Gunsmith."

"This is a rough idea. What do you think?"

"Are you kidding—that's exactly what I had in mind!" Joe blurted out, "When can you start?'

Brad held up his hand. "This is a rough sketch. I'll have a proof ready for you by tomorrow."

Joe's broad smile couldn't hide his excitement. "What time can I stop by to look at the final design?"

"Noon tomorrow."

"See you then." Brad was the first person he'd met who didn't know his life story. *I think I'm going to like Brad.*

When Joe headed back toward his store, a young man with a sheriff's badge was waiting for him.

"Afternoon, my name is Matt Williams. I'm with the sheriff's department."

Joe extended his hand. "Joe D'Angelo. I just moved here from New York." He thought, *He's about the same age as my son.* "What can I do for you?"

"I'm getting a new pistol. Would you mind if I brought it by for you to look at?"

"I'd be happy to—stop by anytime."

Matt's broad smile filled his face. "I've heard you were a big deal cop in New York."

"No, just a patrol sergeant."

Chapter 24

CALLOUSED KNUCKLES

Rachel and Sue spent the evening discussing incorporating Sue's artwork and studio into Rachel's existing business. Finally, they decided to break out the wall separating Rachel's store and the building next door.

Rachel remarked, "I have a tenant in the third store. He's a friend of Kyle Mitchell's. He just moved here from New York." Her eyes twinkled; she thought, *Maybe the two new foreigners will have something in common?*

Sue frowned. "I know that look. I remember that blind date you set up for me with the football player. He couldn't complete a sentence."

"You're too judgmental. This man, Joe, served in the Army with Kyle and just retired from the police force."

"Does he have calloused knuckles?"

"You're too much!"

The friends spent the balance of the evening drawing floor plans for their new combined galleries and gift store. Sue had brought five complete canvases with her and two that were in process. Her easels and supplies were in the living section of the horse trailer.

At seven the following day, the friends were making breakfast and giggling like school girls.

Rachel remarked, "This will be a lot of fun, getting our new business going."

Sue smiled. "No more football players."

When they arrived in town, Rachel squealed, "Look, Kyle's friend is already in his store. Let's go, say hello."

Sue's look could have melted ice. "Is this a setup?"

"No, I swear." Rachel opened the door to the new gunsmith store. "Joe, are you home?"

Joe looked up from behind his new counter. "Good morning, Rachel."

"I'd like to introduce you to my friend Susan Reed. She's moved here from California."

Sue extended her hand. "Nice to meet you. Rachel tells me you're from the Bronx."

"No, I'm from Brooklyn."

"Oh, sorry. Rachel said you're retired from the police force."

"That's correct. I'm going to open a gunsmith store."

"Really?"

Rachel thought, *That's what she said to that football player when he started talking about his sport.* She could tell this conversation was going nowhere. "We have a lot of work to do. Sue's a painter, and she'll be in the store between us."

Joe couldn't resist. "I was thinking of repainting my apartment in the back, and maybe I could hire you."

"I'm not that type of painter." She chuckled and looked at Rachel. "Your knuckles look callused." With that, Sue turned on her heel and walked out of the store.

Rachel's icy glance gave Joe another opening. "I've got an Italian friend in the Bronx; maybe I can have him paint my place and have him help your friend with her work."

Rachel smiled. "Okay, you got me."

"Whatta you mean?" he shrugged like his grandfather had when he played the dumb Italian.

"Have a nice day." Rachel waved as she left.

Chapter 25

THE GUNSMITH SHOP
OPENS FOR BUSINESS

The Night Owl Café

The work on the new shop and living quarters progressed. Joe wasn't ready for a social life and the work was exactly what he needed. Rachel and her friend were okay, and he felt a little guilty about how he had rebuffed them. He glanced at his watch at one o'clock. *No wonder my stomach is growling.*

He'd noticed a restaurant on a side street on his way to town. *What was its name, Owl something?* He locked the shop door and headed toward the café. It was a beautiful day for a walk; the restaurant was three blocks from the store. *There it is; the Night Owl.* The front door conveyed a rustic western look and the inside more than delivered on the promise. A counter supported by cedar beams sat about fifteen feet from the door. The store displayed a wide variety of western decorations and artifacts. Joe approached the counter and noticed a sign that read: *Hi, my name is Rowdy; I'm Canyon's only blind barista. Please help me out and tell me your full name.* Without the sign, you'd never know Rowdy was blind. He turned toward Joe. His face lit up.

"My name is Joe D'Angelo. I'm new in town. Is it too late for lunch?"

"No, sir, you're right on time. What can I get you?"

"Black coffee and a BLT sandwich."

"Have a seat, and I'll get your order ready."

Joe selected a rough-hewn table near a display of western art.

As Rowdy prepared the order, a young girl entered the room.

Rowdy commented, "Janey, say hello to Joe D'Angelo. He's relocated here from New York City, if I got the accent right. He lived in Brooklyn."

Joe chuckled. "That's correct. Someone earlier today accused me of being from the Bronx. To a Brooklyn boy, them's fighting words."

Rowdy called out, "That must have been Rachel's friend from California."

Joe erupted into a belly laugh.

"Hi, Mr. D'Angelo," Janey said as she placed the napkin, fork, and knife on the table.

After lunch, Joe spent a few minutes examining the mounted animals hanging from the walls and the tin roof ceiling. Rowdy was busy working on installing a new doorknob on the front door; he called out, "Walk out the back and go into the small building a few feet from the back door. You'll be surprised."

Joe stepped inside the small building. Two cages lined one wall; a large bird sat in each cage. Joe wasn't sure, but one bird looked like a falcon and the other an owl. He admired the magnificent creatures. It was apparent these were hunting birds. He'd heard about them but had never seen one. Joe walked to the front door. Rowdy stepped aside. "Those birds are something."

Rowdy opened the door. "They belong to my friend Megan who owns the store, and we rent the front."

Joe paused. "How did you know I was from Brooklyn?"

"I'm blind, but my hearing is excellent; I spend my evening hours listening to audiobooks. I've listened to several books by different New York writers, and there are slight variations in accents between the boroughs."

Joe chuckled, "Yeah, someone from Staten Island might as well be from Mars."

Rowdy responded, "The Martians roll their R's."

Joe gave a belly laugh. "You got me."

A grin spread across Rowdy's face. "Y'all come back."

"Count on it."

As Joe walked back to his store, his spirits lifted. He was amazed at Rowdy; he did more without vision than most sighted people did.

Joe's work in his shop was proceeding, and he liked what he'd accomplished. Constructing the counter took half a day. The gunsmith workbench he brought with him from Brooklyn was the same one his grandfather and father used.

He had disassembled it with care and secured it to the floor of the pickup truck's bed.

He had designed the shop so he could work and see the front door. His workbench sat against the wall, the assembly area with the rifle mounting stand facing the store's front. He mounted his collection of screwdrivers; one row was for metric, and the other for U.S. sizes. Different tools, hammers, tongs, etc., were hung for easy access. The new counter was designed to prevent customers from touching the weapons.

Joe purchased second-hand furniture for the apartment in the rear of the building. However, one item he did not skimp on was the security system. The security cameras were placed discreetly inside and outside the building. In addition, Joe replaced the rear door with a steel door mounted on a metal frame.

His final improvement was the beautiful hand-painted sign done by Brad, announcing the purpose of the business: *Gunsmith*. Brad had agreed to paint the window on the weekend. To pay for the window art, Joe had agreed to repair his Winchester rifle.

Rachel stopped in. "That's a beautiful window sign. I bet Brad did it! He's a great artist." Then, she paused. "You and Brad are a lot alike."

Joe was perplexed. "I don't see the similarity."

"You're both loners."

He asked, "Want to see what I've done to your building?"

"Sure."

Rachel was full of praise for Joe's craftsmanship. When they got to the apartment, she asked, "Who was your decorator?"

Without missing a beat, Joe answered, "Goodwill."

Her laughter filled the room. Then she stated, "This back door could stop a Mack truck."

"At heart, I'm still a New Yorker. Money spent on security is never wasted. The new front window is bulletproof."

Rachel shook her head. "Y'all Yankees are sure strange." She smiled. "Sue and I are going to expand my store into the empty place between us. Do you think you could help us?"

"I'd be happy to. We'll agree on the price after the work is complete."

"Good deal."

Chapter 26

COWBOY TRAINING

Joe's repair business grew as gun owners heard of the new service. Joe worked on Rachel's project after closing hours. His days and nights were busy, and time flew by.

Sue and Rachel wanted to have separate studios. Sue decorated her walls with paintings she'd brought with her. She set up her easels and arranged her paints. She typically worked on two or three pictures at one time. Rachel used her space for her pottery.

When Joe's work was finished, Rachel asked Joe, "Is two months' rent payment enough?"

Joe said, "Deal."

His new world was taking shape. The repair work provided a decent income and enough human contact to keep his mind occupied. At night he became reacquainted with his favorite pastime—reading.

Joe spent some of his time off with Kyle; one day, Kyle asked Joe, "Do you know how to ride a horse?"

"You didn't notice that there's a bridle path down the middle of Kings Highway?" Without waiting for an answer, Joe continued, "The owner of the stable at the foot of the path was a friend of my father's, and he let me exercise his horses when business was slow. Most of the rides were peaceful, but sometimes a horse would act up. I can't say I'm a good rider, but I've done some riding."

Kyle nodded. "Okay. We have some well-broke horses. If you'd like to give it a try, you could ride with Jose, my top hand, checking cattle."

Joe answered, "Sure. Why not?" Joe's cowboy training was about to begin.

Early one Saturday morning, a loud knock on his rear door jolted him. Joe looked at the security monitor. He opened the door. Jose was every inch a cowboy: black Stetson hat, blue work shirt, wrangler blue jeans, and a large belt buckle.

"My name is Jose; Mr. Kyle asked me to take you on my rounds."

Joe finished getting dressed. He put on new blue jeans and wore old sneakers; he slipped on his New York Yankees baseball cap. As Joe stepped out the door, Jose looked at his clothes.

Joe said a little defensively, "This is what I wore when I went horseback riding in New York."

Without a word, Jose motioned him to follow. The horses for the day's outing were standing side by side in the front compartment of a gooseneck Easley trailer. As Joe slipped into the passenger seat of the truck, the diesel engine roared to life. Talking over the engine's noise, Jose commented, "The first place we're going to stop is about a half-hour from here." Joe realized that Jose was not a person given to chit-chat.

Jose pulled up to a barbed-wire gate. Joe knew the passenger was supposed to open the gate. The interior door handle didn't work as he tried to open it.

Jose said, "The door opens from outside."

Joe rolled down the window. It took maneuvering, but he got the door to open. He looked at the gate. *Do I have to stand on my head?* The gate was secured with a strand of wire pulled tight to the top of a fence post. His first attempt to remove the wire was a failure. Next, he braced his shoulder against the post and pulled with all his might; the wire sprang open. He pulled it aside and laid the gate down; Jose drove through. Joe reattached the gate and climbed back into the truck. Jose commented, "Maybe I should loosen that fence up."

The road into the pasture was straight and led to a set of pens. Jose parked the truck and walked to the back of the trailer.

Joe noted that the latch to open the trailer door required manipulation. Jose walked to the side of the rig and motioned Joe to follow. He opened the front gate, which divided the trailer into two compartments, and pushed it open. The horses backed out of the trailer. The first horse was a stout roan with a black mane. Jose caught his reins as the horse stepped out.

Jose said, "The bay horse is yours." Jose tied his horse to the back of the trailer. "Mr. Joe, mount your horse." Joe mounted the horse.

Jose held the horse's reins. "How does it feel?"

"Okay."

Jose glanced back at him. "The stirrups are too short." He tapped Joe's leg and removed his foot from the stirrup. Jose slid the stirrup bracket up and dropped the clamp to a lower hole. He placed Joe's foot in the stirrup. Without a word, Jose repeated the same procedure on the other side.

Holding the reins, Jose stood in front of Joe and his horse. "Stand up." Joe made sure his feet were secure and stood.

"Get the balls of your feet under you," Jose directed, and then inspected Joe again. He mounted his own horse. "Let's go."

Joe followed at a slow trot. Jose weaved through mesquite and cedar trees. The brush tore Joe's new blue jeans, and thorns penetrated his sneakers. The cows ignored them.

Jose spotted the calf he was seeking. Joe could tell the infant was sick, with its runny nose and downcast eyes. Slowly, Jose uncoiled his rope. In one swift motion, he roped the ill animal's back legs. Then, Jose said, "Get off your horse."

Jose's horse maintained pressure, dragging the calf slightly. Jose jumped on the frightened animal and held it down on its side. He motioned to Joe. "Hold the front leg up."

Jose adjusted Joe's grip; the calf was powerless. The cowboy removed a medicine bottle and a syringe from his saddlebag. He measured the proper dosage and injected the serum into the calf's rear leg.

"Okay, let her go." He mounted his horse and stroked his mount's withers, relaxing the strain on the rope. The calf scampered away, bawling for its mother. As Jose coiled his rope, he said, "Mount up."

They worked until noon. Joe lost count of how many animals Jose roped and doctored.

Jose looked at his watch. "Time for lunch."

Joe asked, "Are we finished?"

"No." They rode to the parked pickup truck. With the horses secure in the trailer, Jose took an ice chest from the back seat. He handed Joe a bottle of water and a tortilla filled with refried beans. The partners squatted on the shady side of the truck. Joe asked, "What's next?"

"Two more pastures. About twenty sick animals."

"Is this normal?"

"No. It happens when the weather changes."

As the sun was going down, Joe slid out of the truck at the backdoor to his shop. He entered the access code and pushed the back door open. He pulled off his sneakers and extracted thorns from his fingers; he removed his belt and let his blue jeans drop to the floor. He tossed his tattered shirt onto a chair. His eyes closed as he fell on the bed.

The next morning, Joe's cell phone rang; he recognized the number. "Yeah?"

"Well, old buddy, how was cowboying?"

"I have pain in muscles I never knew existed."

"I talked to Jose this morning. He said you might make a hand."

Joe, still groggy, asked, "What does 'make a hand' mean?"

"It'll take a while for you to understand the lingo, but that's about as close as you'll get to a compliment."

Kyle laughed at his joke. "Come over to the house for a late lunch around two. Britta is preparing a meal to celebrate surviving a day with Jose."

It was ten in the morning. Joe said, "It'll take a couple of hours to untangle my legs. After that, I'll be there." Joe stood and began exercises to ease the pain in his legs. He rubbed generous amounts of CBD paste on his legs and back and had two cups of extra strong coffee.

Joe arrived at Kyle's ranch promptly at two. A large pickup truck sat next to a Camry. Joe found a place to park his F-150 and slowly made his way to the door. A hot shower, coffee, Tylenol, and CBD cream had finally got him moving.

Britta opened the door. "Come in here and give me a hug."

Joe wasn't familiar with the west Texas mores; reluctantly, Joe complied. "Gently, please."

Britta's tender hug felt good. She smiled. "Everyone's sitting on the back porch." He followed her. Joe was surprised to see Rachel, a man and woman he hadn't met, and Susan. Sitting next to Sue was Brad, the artist who painted his window sign.

Joe thought, *A good match—two artists; they'll have a lot in common. Maybe the loner has met the right woman.* Memories of Anna, his deceased wife, filled his mind.

Kyle motioned to Joe. "I'd like to introduce you to my neighbors." The rancher stood and extended his hand. "My friends call me Cowboy. Meet my wife, Joanna." He continued. "Y'all must be Joe from Brooklyn?" Joe thought, *This man reminds me of Willy Simmons.*

Cowboy's rough hands surrounded Joe's. "Joe D'Angelo, nice to meet you."

Joe nodded to Joanna. Her high cheekbones and broad smile filled out a round face—long, silver-streaked black hair streamed down her back.

Britta sat in her chair. Kyle reached into a Yeti cooler and extracted a Bud Light. He slid a can of beer to Joe and said, "These are all survivors from riding with Jose." Britta paused. "Except for Cowboy." Cowboy raised his can of beer, as did all the others. A loud cheer erupted from the group.

Plates of barbecue, spare ribs, and potato salad decorated the middle of the table. Kyle distributed more cans of beer.

Brad asked Joe, "How was your day with Jose?"

"He's one hell of a cowboy. He doesn't talk much."

"You just met the man who trained Jose." He tipped his glass toward Cowboy.

Cowboy said, "He was a great cowhand before he met me."

Brad nodded. "Cowboy and Jose are cut from the same cloth." He continued, "They don't waste words and don't appreciate flattery. When they begin to speak Spanish, you know you've screwed up."

Joe smiled at that and said, "I guess I had three strikes." Everyone laughed. He asked, "Is he a citizen?"

Kyle responded, "He's a green card and doesn't want to be a citizen. So Jose works here until the week before Thanksgiving. Then he returns to his family's ranch in old Mexico and comes back to Texas right after New Year's. It works well. By Thanksgiving, the cattle are in their winter pastures. When Jose returns in January, we start getting ready for the spring roundup."

Joe stated, "I liked him. No nonsense."

"He's the top hand," Kyle said and then asked, "Would you guys like to do some real cowboy work?"

Joe looked amused. "What's the pay?"

Kyle laughed. "Drink up."

The afternoon passed quickly, with everyone relating stories from previous roundups. As the party broke up, Rachel announced that Sue and she planned to have an open house on Monday and invited everyone to attend.

As the guests were leaving, Cowboy approached Joe. "I heard you repair rifles."

"Correct."

"I'd like to bring my dad's rifle for you to look at."

"Bring it by anytime. I'm open from nine to noon; I close for lunch and reopen at one."

Cowboy nodded. "I'll see you before the roundup. I like to carry my rifle when I ride."

Joe thanked Britta and waved to the others. *Not a bad bunch. I've got to get more practice riding.* His legs were a little unsteady as he departed for the town.

Chapter 27

COWBOY AND THE FLAT TOP MOUNTAIN RANCH

Joe was working on a rifle when Cowboy entered the store.

"Howdy." Cowboy was carrying a lever-action rifle.

Joe hadn't paid a lot of attention, but Cowboy must have some Negro blood, and his eyes were wide set and almond shaped, hinting at something else. Joe thought, *There's not an extra pound on his muscular body.* Cowboy's handshake was firm without trying to dominate.

Joe looked at the gun in Cowboy's hands and commented, "This looks like an original Henry rifle."

Cowboy nodded. "This rifle was handed down to me by my father. The story goes that my ancestor acquired this rifle at the end of the Civil War and used it for hunting and protection."

Joe ran his hand over the American maple stock and one-piece octagonal barrel. "This is an amazing rifle; it's been well maintained. Do you have any idea what this is worth?"

"Nope. It ain't for sale."

"Don't get me wrong. I've worked on many Henry rifles but not an original. Give me a few minutes to clean up and inspect the rifle. Do you have some .44-40 bullets?"

"Have a box in the truck."

Joe spent a few minutes admiring the rifle and asked, "Do you have time to go to the rifle range? I want to do some target shooting."

Cowboy nodded. "I'll drive."

Joe followed Cowboy to his dually crew cab diesel truck. As he slid into the passenger seat, Joe asked, "Do all ranchers have diesel trucks?"

"Everyone who hauls cattle either has one or wishes they did. These trucks might be loud, but I've hauled twelve thousand pounds of cows up the road out of the canyon."

"Are you talking about the road on Kyle's place?"

"The Palo Duro system is about a hundred and twenty miles long; there are a lot of ranches along the canyon."

"I probably won't be able to see them all, but I'd like to."

Joe was not expecting Cowboy's following remark. "If you'd like, I'll take you to my family's home place at the bottom of the canyon range."

As they set up at the rifle range, Joe suggested, "Let's see how this does at one hundred yards and then at two hundred."

Cowboy remarked, "I've used the Henry to kill coyotes, wild hogs, and deer."

"This weapon was designed for accuracy at two hundred yards. I'm guessing you've taken longer shots."

"In the canyon with all that brush, all I need is two hundred yards. But using the elevation sight, I've dropped a deer at four hundred yards."

It took Joe ten rounds to sight in the rifle. Then, as he handed the weapon to Cowboy, he noticed an engraving on the metal covering above the trigger. Joe asked, "It's hard to see, but I think that says 'Ty'?"

"That was my great, great . . . I don't know how many greats . . . great-grandfather's, and he passed this rifle down along with his name. My son is the next in line for it."

"Everyone calls you Cowboy. What's your real name?"

"Ty is short for Tiberius. My given name is Jones."

"It sounds like you're descended from royalty." Wistfully, Joe continued, "I wish this rifle could talk."

Cowboy said, "Each generation has kept the family bible up to date and it tells our story. This rifle was part of each chapter." Finally, he asked, "What do I owe you?"

Joe thought for a few seconds. "Nothin'. But I'd like to visit your ranch and read your family bible."

Cowboy smiled and said, "It'll be my pleasure."

"What's your ranch's name?"

"The Flat Top Mountain Ranch."

Chapter 28

OPEN HOUSE

The fall weather brought chilly mornings and sunny afternoons.

Joe had his store hours painted on the front door. He was open Monday through Friday from 9 a.m. to 6 p.m. and closed for lunch from noon to 1 p.m. Joe began his day with coffee and toast at 6 a.m., followed by a brisk run. Some days he ran to the college track; other days, he ran along county roads.

At 9 a.m. on Monday, Joe remembered, *The ladies are having their open house.* When he finished reassembling a pistol he had repaired, he headed next door.

The last time Joe visited the store was when he did the renovations. A colorful painting of gifts and artwork overflowing from a cornucopia covered the store window along with a new sign saying, *Rachel and Sue's Art Studios and Gift Shop.* The painter of the window art could only be Brad.

The two artists were talking to customers. Joe walked around, looking at the artwork and gifts for the holiday season. All of Sue's paintings drew his attention, but one piece in particular caught his eye. The abstract aerial view of the high plains with rolling hills and groups of trees was spectacular. He thought, *Abstract art captures the scene better than reality.* As he studied the painting, Sue approached with Brad by her side.

"What do you think?"

Joe stroked his chin and tilted his head. Then he asked with a smile, "Is this hung upside down?" Joe looked at Brad. "What do you think?"

Brad said, "If I could paint like that, I'd stop painting windows."

Joe was on sensitive ground. "I was kidding her because she thought I was from the Bronx."

Sue stepped between the men. "Okay, I'm sorry I said you were from the Bronx. How about a truce?"

Joe smiled. "Okay. I agree to a cessation of hostilities."

Sue grabbed Brad's arm, smiled, and walked toward another customer.

Joe thought, *Well, you've stepped on your lip again. But they belong together. What's that old song? "They're writing songs of love but not for me."*

The store was filling up, and Joe needed to open his shop. Rachel walked over, and Joe greeted her and excused himself, explaining that he had to get back to work.

Chapter 29

CHICO, AKA BUMP STOCK

Canyon, Texas

Chico stood in front of Joe's gunsmith store. Pablo's gun supplier had given him an AK-47, and he wanted to upgrade the rifle to fire like the ones he'd used in Mexico. A gang member was behind him as he entered the shop. Chico approached the service counter, extracted a bump stock from a sack, and laid it on the counter next to the rifle.

Chico looked at Joe. "Can you install this?"

Joe noticed the three stars on the man's wrist. He didn't hesitate. "No."

"Hey man, you're supposed to be a gunsmith."

"I am, but I'm not going to install a bump stock on a semi-automatic. There's no lawful use for this."

"Why not? I pay." Chico smiled, and his gold tooth dominated his smile. He eyed Joe up and down. "I could make you install it."

Chico's partner heard the door open. Cowboy stepped into the store and asked, "Any problem?"

Joe answered, "No. This man is leaving."

Chico grabbed his rifle and the stock, and his face was filled with rage as he exited the store.

Cowboy asked, "What was that all about?"

"Beats me." He thought, *That's the same tattoo that was on the bank robber in New York.*

Cowboy remarked, "I hope he's just passing through. That man's probably a drug dealer."

"I know," Joe remarked. "Thanks for the backup."

Chapter 30

THE DEPUTY

Word spread of Joe's skill and knowledge with weapons. A week after the bump stock incident, Matt Williams with the Randall County Sheriff's Department stopped by again.

His dark hair and youthful look again reminded Joe of his son. Joe set down the gun he was working on.

"Good morning. What can I do for you?"

"The cylinder on my patrol pistol keeps getting hung up." With that, he removed a large pistol from a small knapsack and laid it on the counter.

Joe checked that it wasn't loaded. "You use this on the job?"

"Yes, sir." He pulled out his badge and ID card from his pocket and showed Joe.

"Do you intend to shoot a grizzly bear?"

"No, why?"

"This pistol is a .357 magnum. Same pistol as Dirty Harry used."

"Dirty Harry?"

Joe thought, *He was too young to know Dirty Harry.* "My point is, this is too much gun for patrol. I'm retired from the NYPD. I spent over twenty years on patrol."

"My chief said the pistol was okay."

"The average gun battle lasts about eight seconds; you'll be dead by the time you get this monster out of your holster."

His face reddened. "I didn't come here to be insulted."

"No insult intended, just want to help. You're a new patrolman. I noticed that your ID is only two months old. When I was a rookie, I carried a Smith and Wesson .38 revolver. In my last ten years, I carried a 9mm Glock 22; it has more firepower, and it's easier to handle. I'll be happy to look at your pistol, but you might want to think about trading weapons with a licensed gun dealer."

Joe waved the young man to a chair. "Have a seat." Joe inspected the pistol and found the problem, and it was an easy fix. Joe handed the repaired pistol to the deputy.

"What do I owe you?"

Joe smiled. "No charge. Stay safe." He silently prayed, *Dear Lord, wrap your arms around this young man.*

Later that week, Joe was at the firing range, sighting in rifles. Deputy Williams walked over and said, "I got my new Glock." He handed it to Joe.

"Did you buy this here?"

"Yes, sir."

"Let's go talk to Sarge." Joe led the way to the sales office.

Sarge looked up from a magazine he was reading. He knew Joe regularly used the range to test guns and practice. "What can I do for you?"

"I need you to sell the deputy a proper weapon."

Sarge looked at Williams. "He didn't tell me he was a deputy."

"Okay, take this toy back and get him a Glock 22 Gen 4."

The color drained from the store owner's face. "I have one right here. Call it an even trade."

"No. This little thing that's been prettied up to attract women costs one hundred dollars more than the police weapon. Refund the difference."

"Okay." The gun dealer disappeared into his backroom and returned with the exchange. "Sorry for the misunderstanding."

"Two free boxes of ammunition will be enough of an apology."

"Okay." Contrite, Sarge placed two boxes of cartridges on the counter.

Joe and the deputy walked back to the shooting range. Joe spent time showing the deputy how to load and fire the weapon; Joe asked the deputy, "Where's your holster?"

Matt pointed to the same holster he'd used for the .357. Joe shook his head. "Let's go back to the store."

Sarge cringed as Joe and the deputy walked in. "What now?"

"We need to buy a Black Hawk Epoch holster."

"I think I have one in the back." The dealer hustled into the back room and returned with the holster.

Joe opened the box. "Looks good." He turned to the deputy. "Give him the hundred dollars back."

"Wait a minute. That holster costs more than a hundred dollars."

Joe handed the money to the store owner. "You forgot the law enforcement discount. This young man is out there protecting us." Joe smiled and said, "I'll also tell all my customers what a stand-up citizen you are."

The store owner nodded to the deputy. "Thank you for your service."

Joe showed Deputy Williams how to mount the holster on his belt and how to draw the weapon. The young officer stated, "I don't know how to thank you."

"Practice what I've shown you. That's all the thanks I need."

After that, a steady stream of law enforcement officers stopped at the gunsmith's to ask Joe's advice on weapons and police procedures. His workweek flew by. He smiled as he thought, *Just like working with the rookies at the 81st.*

Chapter 31

MEGAN THE FALCONER

Joe didn't go out to lunch every day, but once or twice a week he enjoyed going to the Night Owl Café and talking to Rowdy. They liked to read the same books. One day as they discussed C.J. Box's Joe Pickett novels, someone entered through the back door. Rowdy called out, "Megan, come up front and meet my new friend."

An attractive, slim woman entered the café. Joe stood to greet her. Megan's blue eyes reflected her smile, and short blond hair framed petite features. Her handshake was firm. She radiated strength. Megan asked, "Do you mind if I have a seat? It's been a long day, and I could use a latte."

Rowdy headed to the coffee station. "Coming up."

Megan said to Joe, "He's told me about you. Is it quite a change from New York?"

"That it is." Joe paused. "I can tell from your accent that you're not from around here either."

"Correct, my father was a career soldier. We moved a lot. He was originally from Montana, and when he had furloughs, we'd visit relatives who lived near Billings."

"What brought you to Canyon?"

"With my survivor's check, I looked around for a place to settle and start a cattle ranch. I purchased some land near Palo Duro Canyon. Before that, I was a game warden in Montana, and I learned a lot about rangelands and what it takes to feed livestock."

Joe asked, "Was your father killed in action?"

"Yes."

"What's your last name?"

"Warlock."

Joe's back stiffened as if he was coming to attention. "Captain Phillip Warlock?"

"Yes."

"Your dad was a legend in the Army Rangers. It's an honor to meet his daughter."

Megan responded, "The honor guard at Dad's funeral in Arlington Cemetery said the same thing; I'll never forget it."

As they talked, Rowdy brought Megan her order. Rowdy sat with them and they changed subjects, talking about their favorite authors and falconry. Megan mentioned that C.J. Box's description of falconers drew her to her hobby.

Megan grew hesitant. "I've got to get going."

Joe answered, "Let's have coffee again." He stood and extended his hand. As their hands touched, he felt something stir in him. *I haven't had that feeling in a long time. Conversation with her is easy.*

Megan's slight smile creased the edges of her mouth as she headed to the back door. She closed the door and said to herself, "Why am I always attracted to military types?"

Chapter 32

THE ROUNDUP

The fall chill brought changes to the color of the leaves and turned the grass brown. On the weekends, Joe helped Jose and Kyle prepare the pastures for winter. They spent long days loading round bales of hay onto trailers and driving them to the appropriate fields. Kyle loaded the trailers, and Jose waited at the winter pasture to unload. Getting the bales near the cows was important, and it was better to do it when the weather was good.

One day, Kyle explained to Joe, "We don't have winters like up north, but bad weather blows in like a freight train going at full speed. I've seen weeks when we couldn't get a trailer down the road. Sometimes we have to use ATVs to get to the cows to spread out hay and break up ice in the water tanks."

Joe's lips curved up. "When we dug in up in the mountains of Afghanistan, you told me West Texas was a tropical paradise compared to that."

Kyle smiled. "It is. Here, if there's a bit of bad weather, don't worry—it'll change."

Joe helped move cows between pastures, working with Jose and Kyle. The old Mexican cowboy accomplished his tasks with unhurried grace; at lunch one day, Joe asked Jose to show him how to use the rope.

"Mr. Joe, take up that spare lariat. Stand next to me and do what I do." Jose placed a barrel about twenty feet away. He circled his head with a ten-foot loop. Jose extended his arm and watched the loop glide over the barrel. He nodded to Joe.

Joe uncoiled the spare lariat and tried loosening up the coil. The loop that circled Joe's head did not look like Jose's; the rope settled around his head. He looked helplessly at Jose.

"You need to practice."

A week before Thanksgiving, Kyle asked Joe, "Would you help gather cows from the ranch land south of Palo Duro State Park?"

Joe said, "Sure. How do you gather them?"

Kyle answered, "I'll drive the feed truck to the last water tank and blow my horn and sprinkle sweet feed. Then, all the riders have to do is follow the cows to the next tank. After the last tank, we put them in that pen at the base of the trail."

Joe responded, "When are you doing this?"

"Next Saturday."

"Okay. But it sounds too easy."

Kyle chuckled. "I'll have Jose pick you up at five on Saturday morning."

"Is the sun up then?"

That Saturday, right on time, there was a familiar rap on his back door. Jose looked at Joe's apparel and said, "I have a pair of chaps you can wear."

Mist shrouded the truck on the way to the ranch. Joe would not have been able to navigate the trip to the top of the canyon.

Jose's steady hand guided the truck and trailer over the cattle guard to the pipe corral with no hesitation.

They were not the first to arrive. Rachel and Sue stood holding the reins of their horses; Kyle motioned toward the ladies. Joe and Jose unloaded their horses and joined the group. Kyle said, "I have to get going; see you down below."

Jose nodded. "Si, jefe." Kyle's truck disappeared into the mist.

Joe pulled on his chaps. "I think I'll warm up my horse."

As other riders arrived, they unloaded their horses, tied them to the corral railing, and joined the congregation near Kyle's truck. The group introduced themselves. Cowboy walked over and stroked Joe's horse. "You're riding a good one."

The group exchanged pleasantries as they waited another fifteen minutes as the shades of gray faded, announcing the coming of dawn. A beat-up pickup truck and trailer exploded out of the mist and screeched to a halt.

A hand jumped out of the cab, followed by several other young men. "We had to air up a flat." Jose motioned Joe to get off his horse.

One cowboy opened the trailer gate. Horses stumbled out; riders grabbed their reins. None looked older than 18, and they were dressed in a variety of cowboy hats. Decorative spurs adorned the heels of their boots. Each tightened their saddle's cinch; with practiced agility, they sprang into the saddle. One horse lowered its head and bucked. The other cowboys whooped and cheered. The horse had a mind of his own and jumped in front of the tied-up horses; they pulled back and broke free. The pitching horse finally gave up. One cowboy commented, "I don't think you made eight seconds. Last time, he threw you." His companions whooped.

Jose held up his hand and mounted his horse. Joe checked his horse's cinch and thought, *What next? A bullfight?*

Chapter 33

WHAT'S NEXT, A BULL FIGHT?

Jose led the group to a trail that disappeared into the mist. Joe was riding with Rachel and Sue. Joe said, "This doesn't look like the road Kyle and I used."

Rachel answered, "I've helped Kyle for years—this is the cattle trail. It looks worse than it is."

Sue spoke up, "There's a lot you didn't tell me when I agreed to come."

Rachel laughed and spurred her horse down the trail. Joe and Sue followed. The twenty-foot-wide sandy trail followed a ridgeline on the left-hand side and a drop-off on the right.

The mist lifted as the sun lit up the eastern sky. Jose rode ahead of the group. Next came the dayworkers. The others trailed. Rachel commented, "Let the others get started." She turned in her saddle. "Sue's horse is not used to this type of terrain. She'll follow my horse; we've been riding together for a while. Joe, your horse, has ridden down this trail many times; relax and give your horse his head."

Rachel led. Sue's horse was tentative but followed her pasture mate. Joe's horse waited until he received a gentle squeeze from his rider, telling him it was time to go.

Joe thought, *Relax, right.* The trail sloped down at a forty-five-degree angle. In the first flat area, Rachel stopped. The other riders stopped at the next rest area. "Let's wait for the others to move." The mist was thick below them. "Jose is waiting for the mist to dissipate." They waited for ten minutes. Finally, below them, the trail's end slowly appeared.

Rachel asked, "You guys okay?" Nervous nods assured her. "Let's go."

As the mist cleared and with the bottom in sight, Joe relaxed. The group assembled at a wire gate. A slight smile at Joe indicated that Jose was happy with the descent. He dismounted, laid down the gate, and inspected the riders as they passed through. Jose remounted and spurred his horse into a high trot. Joe's, Sue's, and Rachel's horses waited for the others to pass.

The terrain was as Joe remembered it, but the view from horseback was breathtaking. Soft sand cushioned the horse's hooves, and Joe enjoyed the ride. Without breaking stride, the crew traversed streambeds and narrow paths up the other side of the canyon. The horse trail went places Kyle's truck couldn't. Up ahead, a covey of quail exploded from the underbrush. Jose's horse ignored them, but not the bucking horse from earlier; that one let his rider know he didn't appreciate the birds. The other dayworkers whooped and laughed. One commented, "You almost made eight seconds." The other cowboys almost fell off their horses laughing.

Rachel was riding next to Joe and commented, "Cowboys enjoy a little excitement when they ride; it's probably that horse's first time down here."

Joe remarked, "I'll keep this horse; no surprises with him."

Rachel remarked, "That's why Kyle gave him to you."

They rode past three windmills. At each windmill, Jose dismounted, and opened and closed the gate. Finally, they reached the last fence. Kyle was waiting for them. He and Jose conferred. Everyone dismounted and let their horses graze. Kyle walked over to Joe. "How's it going?"

Joe answered as he rubbed his horse's withers, "Great."

Kyle looked at the horse. "He's my favorite." Kyle continued, "Jose is going to let the horses rest for half an hour. I'll drive to the first windmill and blow the horn to call in as many cows as I can. Rachel knows the drill. You'll be working with her and Sue."

Chapter 34

CAPTURING THE WILD ONE

Jose mounted his horse; everyone followed.

Rachel looked at Joe and Sue and said, "You two come with me."

Rachel turned her horse to the east side of the canyon. The other riders followed Jose. As they rode the fence line, Rachel explained, "This side of the road is our responsibility. We are to push any cows we find to the first windmill."

She stopped. "Joe, you wait here until you see me start moving. Sue's going to ride to the far side. If we're lucky, we'll be able to see each other as we ride. No matter what, keep heading north until you reach the windmill." Sue arrived at a small hill. It was time to move.

Joe said, "Okay, horse, take me to the windmill." As he rode, he tried to keep track of Rachel. The brush thickened. He wound his way through a thicket and came to the edge of a steep ravine. "Well, how do we get to the other side?" It was as if the horse knew what he said. He moved along the edge of the drop-off until they came to a path down. The horse didn't hesitate. Joe leaned back as the animal slid down the trail.

"What's next?" He spotted the way up on the other side of the crevasse. A light touch on the reins encouraged the horse to bolt up the path; Joe held onto the saddle horn.

"Oh, yeah," he said, rubbing the horse's withers. "You're a good man."

They crested a small brush-covered hill overlooking a dry riverbed. Joe stopped and looked for Rachel. He spotted her and told his horse, "Let's keep going." Below him was a cow with a calf.

Joe looked for Rachel; she'd disappeared.

He spoke to the horse, "I guess it's you and me."

He urged his mount toward the pair. The horse knew the assignment. As they approached, the cow bolted with the calf in her tracks. The horse spun and cut off the escape route. The cow charged up the riverbank, and Joe and the horse followed. "There she is." The horse took off as the cow slid from view. They reached the top as the cow slid down another embankment of a dry riverbed and ran away.

Just then, Rachel and her horse slid down and cut off the cow's escape. The race was on. The two horses didn't need encouragement to stay with the cow. Up ahead, the windmill came into view. The water in the tank drew the cow and calf toward it. Kyle's truck sat nearby with a group of cows munching on range cubes. Joe's cow and calf finished drinking and joined the group.

Kyle smiled as they approached. "By God, you captured old 610."

Joe hadn't noticed the number on the ear tag.

Kyle continued, "Look at that fine calf. I almost shot that old outlaw—now I'm glad I didn't."

Other riders drove a group of cows to the assembled herd. Sue emerged from the streambed and rode to her teammates. "I didn't see anything. It looks like you two found a cow."

The daywork cowboys and the other riders surrounded the cattle, forming a man-and-horse barrier.

Jose circled the cows. As he passed Joe, he nodded and took his position at the head of the herd. The crew crowded the cattle.

Joe remarked, "I guess we have to help."

Sue asked, "What do we do?"

Rachel responded, "Stick with me."

The cows slowly followed Jose and the truck. Not all the animals wanted to go.

Joe exclaimed, "Looks like 610 isn't buying into this." The trio blocked her exit from the herd.

Rachel yelled at the cows, "Move along." Each cowboy had their own yell.

Joe yelled, "Next stop Wall Street, move it." The riders near him smiled.

Joe and Sue joined Rachel as she followed the road. The experienced cowhands spread out into the brush. Rachel spoke, "If we let one cow turn, we'll lose the herd."

Joe spotted 610 heading down a riverbed, two riders on her tail. The trio ran to cut her off. The daywork cowboys dodged and weaved through the thick brush; mesquite thorns tore at their chaps.

Finally, the next windmill came into view. Kyle's truck was there, and he was spreading cattle cubes. The herd pushed through the open gate, followed by the riders. Jose closed the gate as the last rider passed.

Joe looked at Rachel. "That was some ride."

Rachel remarked, "You ain't seen nothin' yet."

"I didn't know you were a fan of Al Jolson."

His comment was answered with a blank stare. *Oh well.*

Chapter 35

SORTING

It was time for a rest. The riders led their mounts to the water tank. The lazy spinning of the windmill drew more water from the ground. Joe wet his hands from the pipe, guiding the water into the tank. He was surprised at how cold it was. It felt good to splash water on his face. Jose mounted his horse, and all followed his lead.

Kyle and his feed truck were the first through the gate. Jose led the cowboys to form a living fence around the herd. The cows slowly followed. Several cows attempted to break through the barbed wire fence and return to the south; 610 led the charge.

Joe and the two women cut off their escape. Their job was to clear the gated area around the water tank and chase the stragglers.

The cowboys bracketed the slow-moving herd. As cows drifted off the road, cowboys chased them back. Several tried to escape. The horses seemed to anticipate their movements.

They crested an arroyo, and several cows bolted for the streambed. Two cowboys gave chase. As the stragglers crossed the streambed, Joe heard a crashing sound. A spirited horse and his rider flew off a bluff, separating as they fell. The horse landed on its side, and the rider landed flat on his back five feet away. Joe spurred his horse and rushed to the fallen cowboy. The cowboy sprang to his feet and ran to his horse and helped it stand up. One of the other dayworkers slid down the steep wall and asked, "You okay?"

The young cowboy led his horse in a circle. "He looks fine."

The dayworker laughed. "That'll take some of the buck out of him."

Laughing, the two young cowboys sprinted after the cows.

Joe rejoined Rachel and Sue. "Did you guys see that?"

Rachel acknowledged, "Yep, those cowboys are tough. Let's get moving."

The herd made one more stop at a water tank—the last before climbing the steep trail.

Chapter 36

THE TRAIL UP

Jose approached Joe and his two partners. "Y'all clear out the pen and bring up the rear."

His eyes settled on Rachel. "Keep an eye on the new guys." Each group of riders received their last-minute instructions.

The first rider who headed up the trail was Cowboy. Rachel remarked, "They're cutting out the lead cow. It's tricky. If they can get her moving up, the rest will follow."

Rachel reminded Joe and Sue, "Okay, guys, time to start pushing the cows. Remember, the slower we go, the faster we get done."

The trio spread out across the pen and walked toward the cows. The reluctant cows slowly followed the leaders. Several cows tried to bolt; the cowboys cut them off and pushed them back on the six-foot-wide trail. It took ten minutes for the cows to make some progress up the trail.

Joe remarked, "Did you catch the number on that cow trying to jump the fence?"

"Yep, 610."

An old barbed wire fence was on the right-hand side; the unfenced left-hand side looked down the canyon. Several cows crowded together, and two of the animals slipped over the side.

Oh my God, Joe thought. Two daywork cowboys turned their horses down the hill and slid after the terrified cows. About one hundred feet off the trail, the cowboys cut in front of the panic-stricken animals. Once the cows had calmed down, the cowboys slowly switch-backed the cows up the steep canyon wall.

Rachel held up her hand and commented, "We need to give the cows more room."

Joe looked up at the line of cows inching their way up. *I wish I'd brought a camera.*

Sue pulled her cell phone from her pocket and started taking pictures. Joe remarked, "You read my mind."

All hands concentrated on their tasks. Joe didn't know how long it would take to push the cows up the trail and herd them to the cattle pens. Slowly and patiently, the cowboys kept the cows moving up. At the top of the path, the crew surrounded the herd.

Joe, Sue, and Rachel reached the summit last. In front, Jose headed for the cattle pens. As the cows entered the enclosure, Rachel swung the gate closed. The riders gathered at the water trough and sat as their horses drank.

From the house, Britta called, "Y'all come and have lunch!"

With saddle cinches loosened, the riders replaced their horses' bridles and mouth bits with halters and tied the lead ropes to the side of a trailer.

Joe patted his horse. "Time for a rest."

Britta smiled at Joe. "How'd you like it?"

"It was great."

"Here's a handy wipe. Fix yourself a sandwich and drink lots of water." Britta had spread out a tablecloth on the bed of Kyle's pickup. The picnic lunch consisted of salads, sandwiches, and fruit. A line formed under Britta's watchful eye.

The groups congregated with their riding partners. The sound of laughter from the cowboys was infectious. "Y'all should have seen that dive off the hill. I think he somersaulted." An orange bounced off the loudmouth's head. "Good throw." Another round of laughter. A first-year young cowboy walked to his truck and removed a can of beer from a cooler.

An experienced cowboy yelled, "No!" The new rider grinned and popped the top.

Jose walked over. "No alcohol allowed while working; here's your pay. Sit in the truck until your friends are ready to leave." The young man cast an eye at Kyle. "You heard him." The other cowboys lowered their eyes and ate in silence.

Kyle sat talking with Cowboy and Jose. Kyle explained that the next task was to sort off the yearling calves. The cows stood in a large pen. At the west end, a gate blocked the entrance to an alley.

Rachel said to her partners, "We've got to block the alley. Cowboy and the dayworkers will sort the calves and drive them to us. Our job is to make sure they don't return to the herd."

Jose assigned tasks to the others, waiting for the yearlings.

Rachel explained, "Cowboy will push the calves toward us. If he yells hold, we are to push the cow out of the alley. Line up behind me on the side of the alley."

His horse took his position without guidance from Joe, and he thought, *I'm glad you know what you're doing.*

Cowboy motioned to the young riders. "Let's get started." He stationed a dayworker at the top of the alley. Joe watched as the cowboys separated the calves from their mothers.

Joe thought, *Those horses have cat-like reflexes.*

The first group of calves passed Cowboy. His horse slowly nudged a reluctant calf with his nose. When the yearlings passed Joe, Rachel, and Sue in the alley, Cowboy returned to his position. Rachel's horse spun around and slowly followed the group. Sue and Joe spread out across the alley. Once the yearling cows were through the gate at the bottom, a ground man closed the gate, herded the calves through a second gate, secured it, and opened the exit gate—ready for the next group.

The sorting was going smoothly; suddenly, a group of calves and a cow burst past Cowboy, and he yelled, "Hold!"

The trio spread across the alley. Joe looked at the cow's number—610. He urged his horse forward as the two ladies blocked the exit.

Joe whispered, "Okay, boy, let's get her out of here." The wiley old cow knew the drill—head fake right, run left. Joe's horse jumped to the side and took up position behind 610. The ladies joined in and pushed the wild cow back to the cattle pen. Someone yelled, "Good cut."

The calves to be shipped bawled for their mothers. The daywork cowboys tied their horses, jumped into the pen, and got behind the calves, pushing and prodding. One animal bolted up the ramp; the others, with some urging, followed. Kyle drove the loaded truck away from the ramp. It took five people to move the ramp aside. Jose motioned for Joe, Sue, and Rachel to mount up. "Get behind the cows and push them down the alley."

The trio entered the pen. Rachel remarked, "We'll take about ten cows down the alley and close the first gate." This task wasn't too difficult; the mama cows were hoping for a reunion with their babies. The gate crew ushered the cows toward the exit. As each cow passed through the gate, Cowboy sprayed fly and tick repellant called Ivomec along the top line of their backs; the freed cows could then return to the lower canyon. Old 610 tried to hurdle the fence without success. Rachel remarked, "You're free until next year."

The roundup crew assembled in the picnic area. Water and Gatorade was their reward for completing the task.

Kyle announced, "Seventy calves are headed for the finishing pens, and twenty-five small calves and one hundred cows are going back to their pasture. Good job."

Cowboy approached Joe. "You were in Mogadishu with Kyle. That was some battle."

Joe responded, "I'll never forget it. What unit were you in?"

"Seal Team Six."

Joe shook his head as he followed Rachel and Sue to put away their horses. Cowboy never ceased to amaze him.

Chapter 37

CONVERSATION WITH WILLY

One evening, Joe was reading a book by C.J. Box. His telephone rang. He looked at the caller I.D.: Willy Simmons.

"Hey, Willy, what's up?"

"We've got some good news. Junior will not go to trial for bank robbery. I knew you booked him as a youth but did you know you got his birthday wrong? When the precinct captain heard about the errors on the booking form, my attorney told me he grumbled something about stupid 'Ities.'"

Joe could not disguise his delight. "You don't say."

Willy continued, "The attorney negotiated to have the charges dropped if Junior would agree to testify against the wounded bank robber. That led the robber to a plea deal."

Joe said, "His record will be clear. He's going to graduate from high school this year, right? So what's next for him?"

"He's signed up for the Marine Corps, contingent upon graduation. He scored a ninety on the ASVAB; the recruiter said that after boot camp, he'd probably go to military intelligence school."

"A jarhead in military intelligence—that's an oxymoron." The two old friends laughed.

Joe added, "He got his brains from Shirley." After Willy stopped laughing, Joe asked, "How's your wife taking all this?"

"She's relieved but worried about our boy being a Marine."

Joe expelled a loud breath. "You know, if we didn't join up when we did, it could have been you or I, buffaloed into trouble."

"I know, but I hope our draft-dodging presidents don't get us into another war."

"Amen to that, brother."

Willy went on. "Are you going to come back to New York?"

"I don't think so. Kyle has introduced me to a lot of people. My gunsmith business is doing well, and I'm learning how to be a cowboy."

"Hop along D'Angelo? If that doesn't beat all. Let's keep in touch. Thank you for helping my son."

"We've been friends for a long time. I can never do enough to repay you for that bullet you got dragging me to safety."

Willy sighed. "Just like growing up in Bed-Stuy. You and I are fighting the world, back to back."

"Thanks for the call. Give Shirley a big hug."

"Ten-four."

Joe disconnected the call and sat staring at his combat medals. *I hope young Willy doesn't get hurt.*

Chapter 38

THANKSGIVING

For Kyle Mitchell and other farmers, Thanksgiving would have to wait. Late November was the time to be on a tractor, planting winter wheat and harvesting corn and cotton. There weren't enough hours in the day. Farmers' wives woke early and prepared breakfast and if their husbands were shorthanded, they drove trucks or tractors.

Britta insisted that everyone take Thanksgiving afternoon off and celebrate the holiday.

Kyle entered the kitchen. "Here, as ordered."

Britta smiled and said, "Go wash up and join our friends in the living room."

Rachel and Susan were busy preparing vegetables.

Brad, Troy, and Joe were enjoying eggnog when Kyle entered the room. "Did y'all drink it all?"

Joe answered, "You missed muster."

Brad stood and poured another glass and handed it to Kyle. "Now you know who your friends are." The men chuckled.

Kyle asked Troy, "How're things at the gin?"

"The cotton dryer broke down, and when I finish eating, I have to get back."

Kyle nodded. "That's bad news. The cotton ginning will fall behind." Kyle's cotton was sitting in the gin's yard, waiting.

"I know. As soon as we finish eating, I'll get back to it."

Joe asked, "Is there something I can do to help?"

"We have to take the unit apart; it requires a strong pair of hands."

"I can do that."

Kyle looked at his army buddy. "There ain't nothing my old buddy can't do."

Britta yelled from the dining room, "Dinner's ready."

The men brought their drinks and the remaining pitcher of eggnog and settled into their chairs.

When the Thanksgiving meal was complete, Troy excused himself. "Britta, that was a wonderful meal, but I've got to get back to the gin."

Joe stood. "I'm going to help Troy."

Britta scowled. "Y'all need to take the rest of the day off."

Troy hugged Britta and said, "I know, but the dryers are down. We'll never be able to process the cotton waiting to be ginned without the dryers working. "

She embraced Joe. "You be careful. That gin is a dangerous place to work."

Chapter 39

THE COTTON GIN

Working in a cotton gin was noisy, dangerous work. The workers were Mexicans who crossed the border and migrated north following the harvest. Many workers obtained farm visas; some just crossed the border. Troy Hammond's gin superintendent, Felipe Garcia, hired and supervised the workers. Troy, like most people in the Texas cotton business, spoke Spanish.

The gin was in a large, nondescript corrugated building. Troy handed Joe a face mask and hearing protection. A middle-aged Hispanic man was standing in front of a panel full of gauges. Troy yelled to Joe, "That's the superintendent."

Joe remarked, "I thought this was a cotton gin. It looks like the control panel NASA uses to launch rockets." They walked toward the control panel.

"Felipe, this is Joe D'Angelo."

"You must be the retired New York police officer."

Joe smiled and grasped the extended hand. *Is there anyone who doesn't know I'm a retired cop?* he wondered. "Nice to meet you."

Troy inquired, "How's it going?"

"Slow. The dryer no work."

"You'll have to work with the wet cotton for a little while. Joe and I will try to fix it."

Troy walked down a hallway between two massive structures. He stopped and pointed at a giant funnel-shaped piece of equipment. "Here we are." He pointed to the rows of bolts holding the unit together.

Joe picked up a ratchet wrench. "Where do I start?"

Troy nodded, "You start on this side, and I'll start on the other side; when we meet, we'll remove the covering and replace the broken dryer."

It took the men four hours to replace the heater. Troy inspected the work. "Looks good. I'll call Felipe and have him meet us at the control panel."

By the time Joe and Troy reached the control panel, Felipe was adjusting the processors. Troy asked, "The heater's working?"

"Yes, we'll be able to get back on schedule by the end of the next shift." The superintendent was adjusting processing speed. His fingers glided over the console as he reset the controls. "Esta bien."

It was midnight, and the next shift arrived. The tired workers headed for their trucks. Felipe told them in Spanish, "Your next shift is at noon tomorrow."

Troy scanned the console; he motioned Joe to follow him. "We're good; let's go." As they exited the gin, Joe noticed activity near the parked pickup trucks. Joe motioned Troy to follow him. As they approached the assembly, Joe recognized his wannabe customer, Bump Stock. He cautioned, "Troy, this looks like trouble."

As they approached the congregation, Troy asked in Spanish. "Hey, fellas, any problem?" The workers looked down and shook their heads; one of them said, "Nada."

Troy turned his attention to the three interlopers and, in Spanish, asked, "Anything I can help you with?"

Bump Stock sneered, "Mind your own business." He squared his shoulders as if he would swing at Troy. The other two intruders made motions as if they would draw concealed weapons.

Joe stepped between Troy and Bump Stock; Joe had his right hand behind his back, and his withering stare made Bump Stock backup. "You and your crew are leaving. Now!"

The three intruders stepped back. Bump Stock, trying to hide his fear said, "Later," and made a gang sign, his thumb and pinky extended. He motioned to his companions to back off. They retreated to a black, low-slung Cadillac and spun out of the parking lot.

Felipe ran from the gin. "What's going on?"

Troy continued in Spanish, "Three suspicious characters appeared to be threatening these men. What's the problem?"

Felipe knew the workers wouldn't talk. "Those pistoleros have some hold over these men. I don't know what it is, but they brought it with them from Mexico. If you call the police, we'll never see these men again."

Joe interjected, "This looks like a mafia shakedown."

Felipe shrugged.

Troy was about to interpret. Joe held up his hand. "I don't need an interpreter."

Troy addressed the group, "Y'all go about your business." The workers walked away. Troy mentioned to Felipe, "Better get back to the gin."

"Si, jefe."

Troy and Joe walked toward their parked vehicles. Troy asked, "You don't have a pistol, do you?"

"It doesn't matter—they thought I did."

"Y'all Yankees are hard to understand."

Joe smiled. "Buenas noches."

Chapter 40

THE HOLDUP

Joe's repair business was getting backed up. He mused, *Maybe I've found a new home.*

Sue and Rachel stopped and asked him to join them for coffee. "Sorry, ladies. My work is piling up."

Rachel saw the waiting line of weapons Joe had yet to start and said, "We'll bring you a cup."

"You're an angel." The ladies waved and headed for the coffee shop.

Joe returned to his repairs. He noticed a black, low-slung Cadillac pull up. Bump Stock and one other entered the store. The driver stayed in the car.

Joe stood. "What do you want?"

Bump Stock sneered as he pulled out a .45 pistol from his jacket. "I'll tell you what I want. We're going to take every weapon you have, and you're going to add that new stock to my rifle."

Bump Stock held the pistol the way gang members think looks cool. He pushed through the counter gate with his free hand. As he glanced down, Joe moved. He grabbed the hand with the extended pistol. He placed his thumb over Bump Stock's hand and twisted.

The robber screamed and dropped the pistol. "You broke my hand!" The other criminal reached to draw his gun; he looked up to see Joe's .38 special pointed at his nose.

"Don't move, or you're a dead man. Both of you on your knees."

Rachel and Sue saw a low-slung Cadillac speed away from Joe's store. Rachel said, "Something's wrong." The two friends rushed into the store. Two Hispanic men were on their knees with their hands laced behind their heads. Joe stood covering them with a handgun.

Rachel asked, "What happened?"

"They tried to rob me," he said, glancing at Rachel. "Do you have a pistol?"

Rachel nodded and removed a .38 from her shoulder bag.

"Keep them covered." He looked at Sue. "Call 911 and tell the dispatcher that we need help."

While Sue was calling, Joe bound the perpetrators' hands with strong plastic ties. Bump Stock whined, "You're hurting me, man."

Joe slapped his head. "You're lucky I didn't kill you."

Two patrol cars screeched to a halt in front of the gun-smith shop. A patrolman and the police chief burst through the door, weapons drawn. The chief barked at Rachel and Joe. "Place your weapons on the counter and back off."

Rachel and Joe each placed their weapon slowly on the counter and stepped back, watching the two perps.

The patrolman guarded the prisoners. The chief motioned Joe to follow him. Once out of earshot, he asked, "What happened?"

"I'll show you." The chief followed Joe into his living quarters. He replayed the attempted holdup.

"Did you get the license plate of the driver?"

"Better than that." Joe cued the system to show the car speeding away.

The chief keyed his shoulder-mounted microphone. "We're issuing a BOLO alert. Suspect is armed and dangerous."

The "Be on the Lookout" was automatically broadcast to all law enforcement officers within a hundred miles of Canyon.

Chapter 41

THE YOUNG DEPUTY

Deputy Matt Williams sat in his patrol car south of Canyon. There had been recent complaints of excessive speed from residents. The deputy thought, *Time to slow this road down before someone gets hurt.* A low-slung black car sped by at almost one hundred miles per hour, according to the radar readout. Williams screeched out of his hiding place and keyed his two-way radio, "I've got a black lowrider doing a hundred miles an hour."

The dispatcher cautioned, "We have a BOLO Alert for a vehicle matching that description. I'm going to route you to Canyon's police chief."

"Deputy Williams, this is Chief Clark. Don't attempt to pull the vehicle over. I'm in contact with the sheriff's department and the DPS. Maintain a safe distance."

"I can take this sucker."

The chief ordered, "Deputy, back off! We're going to block the highway south of Tulia. Other units will join you. Is that clear?"

"Yes, sir." Chief Clark disconnected the call. The chief looked at Joe. "Deputy Williams is going to be a fine officer."

Joe nodded. "If we can keep him alive."

Two cars from the Tulia Police Department stopped all traffic from entering the interstate. Police cars blocked traffic in all directions. The State Police placed spike strips across the highway.

Deputy Williams contacted the police chief. "I have the barrier in sight."

The chief responded. "Coming up on your six are two highway patrol cars; slow down and follow their lead."

Disappointed, Williams answered, "Yes, sir."

The fugitive's car hit the spike strips, tires exploded, and the car spun out of control into the median. In a flurry of grass and dirt, the car ground to a halt. Deputy Williams bolted ahead, determined to apprehend the fugitive. He pulled his patrol car into the median and jumped out. From behind the patrol car's door, he leveled his Glock at the disabled vehicle. He yelled, "Get out of your car with your hands on your head!"

"No way, gringo." The fugitive leveled his AK-47 at Williams and sent a volley of bullets into the deputy's car.

The Highway Patrol sergeant, who was following the deputy, engaged his loudspeaker. "Stand down, Deputy." He turned his attention to the perpetrator. "You in the Cadillac, drop your weapon!" Another burst of gunfire aimed at the trooper was the answer.

Deputy Williams aimed his Glock at the perpetrator, who was spraying bullets in all directions. D'Angelo's instructions echoed in his ears. *Never rush a shot.*

The criminal kept the police officers pinned down but didn't notice the deputy's pistol protruding from the shattered patrol car's window. He keyed his radio. "I have a shot. Everyone stay down." He slowly squeezed the trigger, aiming at the fugitive's chest. The shot echoed, and the perpetrator's arms flew out as he fell to the ground.

The other officers rushed the downed fugitive. His lifeless body greeted them.

The cleanup of the crime scene took several hours. While it was in progress, the police chief motioned to Joe, and said, "Let's take a ride."

The Canyon police chief parked next to the sheriff. The sheriff was talking to Deputy Williams.

As they approached, the sheriff said. "Williams, your shot-up cruiser is going to be picked up by a wrecker. Give me your shield and pistol. Ride with the wrecker back to town and go home. Now go sit in your cruiser and wait for your ride."

Dejected, Williams retreated to his bullet-ridden car. The sheriff spotted Joe and the police chief, walked over to them, and said to the chief, "I heard all of the instructions. That kid has too much courage."

The chief agreed. "He needs to be reined in before he gets himself killed."

A slight smile broke the frown of the sheriff. "That was a hell of a shot." He looked at Joe. "You need to keep helping these young officers. The chief and I will put the fear of God in them."

Joe walked over to Deputy William's car. The downcast young man looked up at Joe.

"I killed that man. What was I thinking?"

"You're going to have to puzzle that out. When you're ready to talk, come see me."

Chapter 42

CHRISTMAS SEASON

A week before Christmas, Joe was having lunch at the Night Owl Café. He and Rowdy were discussing a character in a C.J. Box book. Joe remarked, "The falconer has a mysterious past. He is running away from something."

Rowdy objected, "The reader never knows what he did."

They hadn't noticed Megan enter the back door after she fed her raptors. She listened to the conversation taking place. Megan called out, "How about a latte?"

Rowdy exclaimed, "Coming up."

Megan acknowledged Joe and said, "Isn't that the same argument you two were having last time I saw you?"

Joe frowned and said, "We were having a discussion."

"It didn't sound like it."

Rowdy set the latte in front of Megan. "We read the same books."

She laughed. "Box is never going to disclose all of the falconer's past. That's what keeps you buying his books."

Joe asked, "How many of his books have you read?"

"Twenty-one."

Rowdy commented, "Great minds think alike."

Joe couldn't let that comment pass. "So do people in insane asylums."

Rifle repair work never seemed to slack off. Joe walked back to his shop. *Fall is definitely in the air. I wonder how much winter there is in Texas?* He was opening the door as a man dressed in a business suit approached.

"Howdy, my name is Jason Fulbright. I'm the president of the Community Bank."

Joe extended his hand. "Joe D'Angelo, nice to meet you." Fulbright's hand felt clammy. He was an average-sized man, five feet and ten or eleven inches tall. His manicured fingernails and soft hands had never done hard work. He had a slight build and stood erect. His wrinkled skin and graying blond hair made it difficult to pin down his age. His eyes were in constant motion.

Joe asked, "How can I help you?" Fulbright followed Joe into the store and waited until Joe was behind the counter. While he waited, Fulbright's eyes darted around the store. Joe felt uneasy but repeated, "How can I help you?"

"I'm looking to purchase a handgun. What do you recommend?" He continued to appraise the store.

"I don't sell weapons; all I do is repair them. You might want to go out to the retail store at the rifle range. They sell handguns."

Fulbright managed a weak smile. "I was hoping you had something you could sell me. I've heard that gunsmiths sometimes make private sales." He concluded this comment with a wink.

"Not this gunsmith."

"You have a northern accent."

"So I've been told. Is there anything else?"

"No. Thank you for your time." Fulbright's weak smile disappeared. His shifty eyes were trying Joe's patience.

"Okay." Joe motioned toward the door. As Fulbright closed the door, Joe thought, *That conversation didn't make sense. Maybe I'll ask Rachel about him.*

He returned to work on the rifle he was repairing and said aloud, "You're getting paranoid." He chuckled to himself as he recalled Cue Ball Kelly winking when he suggested a friendly game of eight ball with a small bet of five dollars.

That night he was sitting in his apartment reading. His cell phone rang. He didn't recognize the number, but it didn't look like a scam call. "Hello?"

"Joe, this is Rowdy. My mom and I were thinking that if you didn't have anything planned for Christmas day, maybe you'd like to come to our house for dinner?"

"I appreciate the invite."

"We've also invited Megan. We can continue our discussions."

"Did you tell her you were going to invite me?"

"Yes."

"I'd love to come to dinner. What time? And what can I bring?"

"Dinner will be at noon." Rowdy's voice brightened. "Bring whatever you want."

"I'll bring dessert." His mind raced. *I've got to bring something special.*

Chapter 43

TAKE THE CANNOLIS

Christmas was always a joyful time for Joe when he was with his family. Since the death of his wife and son, Joe volunteered for duty on holidays. The other sergeants could spend the holiday with their families, and Joe didn't have to sit at home staring at his service revolver. He knew the Catholic Church forbade suicide. But the holiday season was empty for Joe.

The thought of spending Christmas with Rowdy and his mother felt good, and seeing Megan excited feelings he thought were dead. He knew what he wanted to bring—Italian cannolis. He called several bakeries in Amarillo; the stores didn't know what he wanted. One store clerk asked, "Can what?" Not deterred, he looked up restaurants in Lubbock. His second call was to Orlando's Restaurant, and the manager had a distinct New York accent. Joe asked if they sold cannolis.

"We serve it as dessert."

"Would you sell some?"

"Where you from?"

"Brooklyn."

"For you, I'll sell some."

"When can I pick it up?"

"When you get here."

Joe hung up and headed for Lubbock. Walking into Orlando's was like walking into a New York Italian restaurant. The smell of garlic simmering in tomato sauce reminded him of his family's sumptuous holiday meals. The black and red wallpaper and tables reminded him of a restaurant in Brooklyn.

The owner greeted him as he walked in, "Yo, Joey from Brooklyn. Tony Orlando, nice to meet you."

"This place reminds me of home."

The two talked for a while about New York. It turned out that Orlando's uncle had retired from the New York Police Department; Orlando called out, "Uncle Frank, come here. Meet Joey from Brooklyn, also retired from the NYPD. Let's sit and have a glass of wine."

The conversation finally ended when Joe announced, "This has been great, but I've got to get back to Canyon. I don't want to get a ticket for DUI."

Frank smiled. "It's nice to meet you and talk of the old times. The city we grew up in is long gone. I hope you find a good life out here."

"I'm working on it."

Orlando blurted out, "If it doesn't work out up there, you come here!"

Frank laughed, "Whadda ya know?"

Joe answered, "Get outa here."

Joe started for the exit. Orlando yelled out, "Take the cannolis!"

The Godfather movie line brought uproarious laughter from the men; customers stopped eating to enjoy the laugh. The effect of the wine and the rich conversation with fellow former New Yorkers brightened Joe's mood. He hadn't felt this relaxed in years.

Chapter 44

CHRISTMAS DAY

Rowdy and his mother lived north of town in a small development not far from West Texas A&M. Joe was familiar with the area. He'd run laps on the track. He arrived at noon, and Rowdy opened the door and smiled. "Come in, Joe, almost time to eat."

Joe was amazed at how Rowdy's blindness didn't limit him. During one of their afternoon discussions at the Night Owl Café, Joe commented on Rowdy's ability to function. Rowdy explained, "You've only seen me in this cafe. It took several weeks to master my movements. Mom and I worked on the design so I could work the cafe with the help of a server."

Joe commented, "I've seen you serve customers."

Rowdy laughed, "Yeah, but don't move the chairs."

He led Joe through a hallway to the living room. Megan and Mrs. Milstead, Rowdy's mother, were seated in matching embroidered straight-back chairs. The chairs coordinated with the furniture in the room, and cherrywood end tables bracketed an embroidered sofa. A fireplace was the focal point of the room. As Joe and Rowdy entered, the ladies stood.

Mrs. Milstead extended her hand. "Nice to meet you. Rowdy has told me a lot about you." Joe could detect a mild New England accent.

Joe remarked, "Don't believe him." Mrs. Milstead's bright smile warmed the room.

Megan smiled and said, "Glad to see you. What's in the bag?"

"Dessert."

"What is it?"

"A taste of Italy. You'll see after dinner."

Mrs. Milstead added, "It's time to eat. Shall we go to the dining room?"

Joe admired the wall coverings as they walked to the dining room. The room's table and chairs continued the theme of the living room. A Victorian dining room table with straight-backed dark oak chairs sat under a gold and crystal chandelier. White wood trim surrounded the doorway and the windows and complemented the off-white walls. The table setting was elegant, with forks, spoons, and knives placed correctly. China dishware and sterling silverware sat on a textured white table cloth. Joe thought, *This isn't like other homes I've been to in West Texas. It reminds me of home.*

Mrs. Milstead directed the seating. Joe and Megan sat facing her and Rowdy. The meal consisted of turkey with gravy, mashed potatoes, fresh peas, and dinner rolls. A vegetable salad was the first course; salad dressing sat on the table.

After everyone was seated, Joe addressed Mrs. Milstead. "I detect a northern accent."

"Yes. I'm originally from Boston."

Megan added, "We're a bunch of displaced refugees."

After they finished eating, Mrs. Milstead said, "You go into the living room while I clear the table." The dinner companions ignored their host's order, and all pitched in clearing the table.

Rowdy and his mother set a crystal tumbler and matching glasses next to the box containing the dessert.

Joe announced, "The surprise dessert." He opened the box. Megan's brow wrinkled. Joe explained, "These are genuine cannolis." The box contained twelve tube-shaped shells of fried pastry dough filled with sweet, creamy ricotta cheese.

Each person selected one of the strange-looking pastries. Mrs. Milstead announced, "Let's see if the plum wine goes with this treat."

Rowdy ran his hand over the pastry as Megan took a tentative bite. The empty box sat on the table an hour later, next to the half-empty tumbler of plum wine. A satisfied sigh from Megan signaled that the surprise was well received.

Chapter 45

TROUBLE COMES FULL CIRCLE

Juarez, Chihuahua, Mexico

During the trip from Canyon, Fulbright's thoughts were on his meeting. *I must explain to Pablo Jimenez that his captain is dead, and two of his soldiers are in jail.* The border crossing took an hour of waiting and a brief conversation with a Border Patrolman. Fulbright's false passport worked, as it always did. Twenty minutes brought him to the enclosed, guarded compound of the new leader of the Juarez Cartel. Armed guards inspected his passport, and one of them stepped away and dialed a number known only to Jimenez's organization's trusted members.

Fulbright pulled into a parking space, and two armed guards approached. Practiced hands patted him down. The guards opened the false bottom of the trunk and removed the suitcase full of cash. Fulbright clenched his teeth and grabbed his elbows. *How did I get myself into this?*

What started as a little extra money grew until the cartel controlled him. Fulbright knew that any misstep on his part would put his family in danger. *When Pablo kills someone, he also kills their family.*

"Follow me."

Pablo Jiminez sat in his sparsely furnished office. The guards placed the suitcase on his desk and opened it.

Pablo's eyes narrowed at Fulbright. "That's all you brought?"

A chill coursed down Fulbright's spine as he explained the recent events in Canyon. The men sent to start the drug ring had recruited only two or three dealers.

"Jefe, your men decided to hold up a local gunsmith, who is a retired New York City cop. The leader of the crew got killed in a shootout. The other two were arrested." Fulbright wiped the sweat from his hands and brow as he waited for Pablo to speak.

The cartel leader said, "Tell me about this gunsmith."

Fulbright forced his hand to stop shaking. "The gunsmith's name is Joe Dangle."

Pablo paused. "Spell his name."

Fulbright answered, "D-A-N-G-E-L-O, D'Angelo. Sorry, I pronounced the name wrong."

Pablo's shark-like gaze settled on Fulbright. "I know of this man—he has a debt to pay. Once that gunsmith is out of the way, I'll send some of my best men to get the business going."

Pablo picked up a knife-shaped letter opener and spun it between his forefingers. "We've got to take care of business."

Jose enjoyed being home with his family. The money he earned working for Kyle Mitchell kept the family ranch operating. His father and his brothers were partners, and each year the cow herd increased. Since arriving home at Thanksgiving, his days were spent branding cattle, doctoring sick animals, and cutting out yearling calves for sale.

Jose's brother Oscar mentioned, "Since the police arrested El Chapo, there's been many killings. A new leader, Pablo Jimenez, eliminated all challengers." Oscar shook his head. "It's good that the family has avoided the gangs."

Jose said, "I know our cousin, a soldier in the gang, has protected us. I've seen some pistoleros around Canyon, Texas. What are they up to?"

"Our cousin thinks the cartel is opening new territory. Pablo is mad because one man was killed, and two men are in jail. He thinks that Pablo is going to send an assassin to Canyon and eliminate the problem."

Jose asked, "Did our cousin mention anyone?"

Oscar nodded, saying, "He mentioned some retired New York City police officer. He said that the same policeman killed Pablo's brother in New York City."

Jose's face remained impassive. It was in his family's best interest to maintain good relations with the cartel, but Jose thought, *Somehow, I've got to warn Joe.*

"I'm heading north in a week. It looks like our cattle are doing well."

Oscar's face dropped. "I wish you could come home permanently."

Jose put his arm around his little brother. "Soon."

Chapter 46

FIRST DATE

The Night Owl Café, the week between Christmas and New Year's

Megan entered the aviary to feed her raptors. She finished throwing dead mice in the cages and watched the birds attack their meals. Then, she thought, *A latte sounds good. Maybe that good-looking retired cop will be there.*

As she entered the coffee shop, Joe's face lit up. "Megan, join us."

She smiled. "I wonder if the birds would enjoy cannolis?"

Joe chuckled. "I'll bring them some. Maybe they're Italian."

Rowdy said, "I guess we're now honorary Italians."

Megan settled in her chair and looked at Joe. "How do you like horseback riding?"

"I enjoy it. But I wish I had started riding years ago; Jose told me that I need more time in the saddle."

"I don't think I mentioned it, but I've purchased the riding stable in Palo Duro Canyon State Park. The former owner has let the place go, and the horses need riding before the next season. I've got to evaluate each horse and replace the ones that are too old. I plan to ride each horse a couple of times a week. Are you interested in helping?"

Without hesitation, Joe responded, "I'd love to help."

"Our winters are mild; it usually gets colder in January and February, and it's not unusual for a bright sunny day to follow a blizzard. We'll have to watch the weather and plan accordingly."

"I think I can keep up with my repair business. Maybe we could ride on Wednesdays and Saturdays."

The day after New Year's was bright and sunny. The weather forecast predicted temperatures to reach sixty degrees.

Megan called Joe. "Are you available today?"

"Give me an hour. Do you want me to meet you at the park?"

"I'll pick you up."

"I'll be ready."

Joe placed a sign on the door that he'd be closed for the rest of the day. He selected a clean pair of blue jeans, his new cowboy boots, and his Stetson hat. He had purchased a riding jacket and a blue work shirt. Megan's truck stopped in front of the store. Joe walked to the truck.

Next door, Rachel yelled, "Sue, come here! It looks like Joe's made a friend."

As she drove, Megan remarked, "One thing I like about this area is the winter doesn't settle in like an unwelcome guest. Of course, we'll have some snow and occasionally ice, but it doesn't last; the canyon provides shelter from the wind."

Joe nodded and said, "Tell me about the riding stable."

"The people who owned it wanted to retire. They had it for sale for nearly a year. It's a tough sale. All you're buying is the right to operate a lease from the state of Texas for a term. I was able to get a five-year extension on the existing lease. Included in the sale were the horses and the tack. The state owns the office, corrals, and riding trail."

The drive from the park entrance to the stable took fifteen minutes; the distance on the steep winding road was a little over three miles. It was impossible to drive over ten miles an hour down the narrow switchback. Joe admired the view. "This is a beautiful place."

Megan answered, "That it is. Once we warm up two of the horses, we'll ride the trail."

"Can I help?"

"First, you watch."

The riding stable parking lot, capable of holding thirty vehicles, was empty. She parked in the spot reserved for the owner. "Let's go in. I'll show you the setup."

Behind the counter was an open area filled with saddles on stands with halters and bridles neatly hung from wooden pegs. "I want to work the horses before we go riding."

Joe was uncertain what Megan was talking about but said, "Okay. You'll tell me what you want me to do."

Megan selected two headstalls and a three-foot stick with a rope on its end. Joe followed her to the corral. "Wait here." She opened the gate, entered the corral, and closed the gate behind her. She walked over to a sorrel mare, stroked her neck, slipped the halter over the horse's nose, and fastened the strap under its neck. "Okay, Daisy, we're going to have some fun."

She led the horse through the gate and handed the lead rope to Joe. "I'll be back." She reentered the corral and selected a roan gelding. As she exited the corral, she said, "This is Oscar." She led the horse to a thirty-foot round pen. "Watch how I warm him up."

She led the horse into the pen and removed the lead rope. Oscar stood while Megan walked to the center of the arena. She set her feet, pointed with her left hand, and struck the ground with her training rope and stick. Oscar trotted around the pen. The horse made five revolutions; Megan stepped to her left, switched hands with the rope stick, and held up her right hand. The horse turned around and trotted in the other direction. After another five revolutions, Megan dropped her arm and placed the rope stick in front of her. The horse stopped, looked at her, and slowly walked over to Megan. Megan walked to the gate and attached the lead rope. She stroked the horse's withers. "This horse and the one you're holding are well trained. This exercise teaches the horse to move its feet on command."

Joe asked, "I guess you want me to do the same thing with Daisy?"

Megan smiled and said, "You catch on fast."

Joe led Daisy into the circular pen, mimicked Megan's actions. Joe stood in the center of the round pen, lifted his left hand, and pointed. "Well, look at that." Daisy trotted around in the direction he pointed.

Megan encouraged, "Good, keep your arm pointed and let the rope whip drag on the ground as you turn and follow her trot, and then drop your arm."

Joe counted the revolutions aloud. When he reached five, he asked. "How do you turn her?"

"You're doing great. Let the horse pass you one more time." Daisy trotted by. "Okay, drop your hand, move to the left and cut her off. Then, shift the rope stick to your other hand and point your right hand in the other direction."

Joe thought, *I hope Daisy knows the drill.* As the horse approached Joe, she spun on her hind legs and trotted in the other direction.

Megan directed, "Get back in the middle."

Five more revolutions completed, Joe looked at Megan. She said, "Drop your arm, rest the stick in front of you and relax your shoulders." Daisy stopped, turned toward Joe, and slowly walked toward him. Joe stroked Daisy's long face and neck, saying, "That's a good girl."

Megan laughed. "That was lesson one."

Megan and Joe led their horses to a hitching post. Megan said, "Let's sit and talk. I brought a thermos of coffee."

They sat and admired the beauty of the canyon. Joe watched two hawks circle. Megan poured the coffee, "You have a good feel for horses. I need help getting the other horses as well trained as Daisy and Oscar. There are some other basic movements I want to show you. Then we'll ride the trail."

Megan explained how to flex a horse's neck. "With a gentle touch, the horse should bend its head toward the side of the pressure." She demonstrated on Oscar. Joe repeated the move on Daisy.

Joe asked, "Why do this? I thought if you pulled on the reins in one direction, it automatically turns?"

"Every movement you ask the horse to do has to be trained." She gently lifted Oscar's left rein; his head snapped around. "I want the horse to turn with the minimum amount of effort."

"That makes sense."

"Let's saddle our horses and inspect the riding trail."

"Sounds like a plan."

Joe and Megan spent Wednesdays and Saturdays working with the horses.

After each session, they rode the trails. One day there was a light dusting of snow. It was a bright clear day; the wind was calm. Megan and Joe thought it would be a good day to ride.

Joe remarked, "The snow turned this beautiful land into a dream world."

Megan smiled. "You have a way with words."

Chapter 47

MATT MEETS ROWDY

Deputy Williams stepped into the gunsmith store. Joe looked up.

"Good morning, Matt, how have you been?"

Matt looked at the floor. "Okay, I guess. The sheriff has reinstated me."

Joe didn't like that answer and asked, "Let's take a walk."

"Okay."

Joe locked the front door and motioned Matt to follow him. "Let's go to the Night Owl Café for coffee."

Matt stated, "I've driven by there several times but never stopped."

As they entered the coffee bar, Rowdy turned to face them.

"Good morning, Joe. Who's this with you?" He extended his hand.

Matt realized that the extended hand belonged to a blind man. He gripped Rowdy's hand. "I'm Matt Williams."

"What can I get you?"

Matt looked at Joe. "We'll have two of your special lattes." The store was otherwise empty. Joe sat at his regular table.

Rowdy brought the steaming beverages and asked, "Do you mind if I join you?"

Joe answered, "That would be great."

Rowdy began the conversation. "Deputy Williams, I read about that terrible shooting. How are you handling it? Oh, I get my newspapers in braille."

"I suppose you know I acted stupidly."

Rowdy turned to face the deputy. "That's not the way I see it." Matt looked quizzically at Joe.

Before either could speak, Rowdy smiled. "Don't misunderstand; I see it in my mind's eye." Rowdy folded his hands. "The morning of the holdup, three Hispanics stopped here for breakfast. I overheard their conversation. They spoke Spanish, and like most sighted people, they think because I can't see that I'm also deaf. The last thing they expected was a white blind guy who spoke their language."

Joe asked, "What did they speak about?"

"How this town would be an easy place to take over. I wasn't sure what they were talking about and didn't ask." Rowdy laced his fingers and tapped his thumbs. "When I heard about the robbery, I put two and two together. They did mention that an Anglo cop might be a problem." Rowdy continued, "It turns out that the fellow Deputy Williams shot was a well-known Mexican gangster and had vowed never to spend time in an American jail. Rumor has it that after the United States imprisoned El Chapo, a war settled which gang controlled pieces of El Chapo's empire, and the new drug lords are trying to secure their areas."

Matt asked, "How do you know that?"

"Before my accident, I was with the Drug Enforcement Administration. I keep in contact with my old buddies." He faced Matt. "DEA agents are frustrated by bureaucracy; they know something is going on, but they can't tell the local police. It took me a couple of weeks to piece this together."

Joe interjected, "You're the only other person who knows this. Don't betray Rowdy's confidence." He sighed. "We don't know what's next."

Matt spoke, "I guess I didn't do so badly after all."

Rowdy frowned. "Your action almost got you killed. I know what I'm talking about; a lot of young officers get injured because their testosterone overrides good sense." He chuckled. "I'm living proof."

Megan opened the back door and walked to the seated trio. "Hi, guys, can I join you?" Without waiting for an answer, she sat down. She smiled at Joe and asked, "Who's this handsome young man with you?"

"Matt Williams, meet Megan Warlock." Matt stood and extended his hand.

"You look about the same age as my niece; when she comes to visit, I'll introduce you to her."

Joe thought, *I didn't know she had a niece. There's a lot I don't know about Megan.*

They ordered lunch and sat talking; finally, Joe said, "I've got to get back."

On the way back to Joe's shop, Matt commented to Joe, "I wish I'd known about this before."

"It took Rowdy a few weeks to piece this together. I was hoping you'd stop by."

A frown knitted Matt's brow. "I don't know if you've heard, but the two robbers have a high-powered Dallas attorney. We're holding them on an attempted robbery. They're illegals. My boss suspects that the attorney will make a case for returning them to Mexico and letting the Mexican government hand out the punishment." Matt continued, "The sheriff thinks the overworked judge will be happy to get this case off his calendar."

Joe smiled sadly. "We'll have to see what happens." Joe placed his hand on Matt's shoulder. "I'm glad you decided to stick with law enforcement."

Joe's smile disguised his thoughts. *This isn't over.*

Chapter 48

ANOTHER ROUNDUP
AND WOMEN

The months of January and February were busy for Joe. His friendship with Megan deepened.

Rachel burst through the gun shop door at coffee time, with Sue right behind her. "You've got to join us today."

Joe looked up. "My pleasure."

The coffee crew was already seated as Joe and his female companions joined them. Troy Hammond greeted Joe and said, "The heater didn't miss a beat; ginning is complete."

Joe responded, "That's an impressive operation. I'm glad I had a chance to see it."

Kyle entered the coffee shop and pulled up a chair. "The normal suspects are present; saves me a bunch of phone calls. In two weeks, we've got to work the ranch I lease north of Turkey. I need y'all's help."

Joe and Sue looked at each other; Joe asked, "A few details, please."

Kyle answered, "It takes two days to work the ranch. It's too far to travel back and forth. Jose and Cowboy will set up camp Friday afternoon. You'll have to bring your sleeping bag."

Rachel could see the confusion on Sue's face. "There will be separate tents for the men and the women."

J.C. Sparks beamed. "That ain't no fun."

Rachel's elbow dug into J.C.'s ribs. He grinned and yelled, "Ouch!"

Joe asked, "I'd like to invite Megan. She's a great rider."

Sue and Rachel exchanged knowing glances.

Kyle spoke, "I'd like to meet her. Rumor has it there's a budding romance."

Joe turned pale. "We're just friends." Sue and Rachel burst into laughter.

In the second week of March, the local television station forecasted a sunny day with temperatures in the mid-sixties.

Kyle contacted Joe. "Are you still planning to help this weekend?"

"I'm looking forward to it. Megan agreed to come, and she wants to bring two of her horses. She thinks the work will be good for them."

"That's great. We'll assemble at my house at 5 a.m. and drive to the ranch."

Joe sighed, "Just like boot camp."

Kyle laughed, "Remember, separate tents."

Joe scowled. "I told you we're just friends."

"Right."

The day before the roundup, Joe and Megan picked up their mounts. At Kyle's house, they turned the horses out in an empty paddock. Britta joined them. "You must be Megan. I'm Kyle's wife Britta, and if you don't mind, I'll ride with you to the ranch tomorrow."

Megan nodded. "Sure, we'll see you tomorrow morning."

As Megan exited the truck, Joe said. "I'll pick you up at 4:30."

"Okay. What have you told your friends about me?"

"Only that you're a friend."

She inspected Joe. "Hmm, see you in the morning." Then, she turned on her heel and headed to her house.

As Joe headed to town, he thought, *Women.*

Chapter 49

COWBOY CAMP

Joe and Megan arrived at Kyle's house a few minutes before 5 a.m. Overnight, the temperature had fallen to forty degrees. The weather forecast was for a sunny day and temperatures to reach sixty-five degrees.

Arena lights illuminated the horse stalls. Britta greeted Joe and Megan. "Here's some coffee for the trip. These two ladies are Rachel Meadows and Sue Reed. They've already loaded their horses."

After introductions, Britta stated, "Time to get your horses loaded and be on our way. Rachel knows the way; we'll follow her." Britta smiled and said, "I'll ride with you—just in case."

Oscar and Daisy stood at the gate as if they were waiting for their riders. Joe and Megan slipped halters around the horse's heads and led them to the trailer. They secured the horses. Megan exclaimed, "We're ready to go."

Britta walked to Megan's truck's passenger side and motioned for Joe to sit in the back seat. Rachel and Sue sat waiting in their vehicle. Britta said, "I've got to turn off the arena lights." The lights from Megan's truck illuminated Britta's path to the light switch.

Britta settled into her seat. "Rachel knows the way; we'll follow her."

They all sipped their coffee in silence. Megan concentrated on following Rachel's truck. Britta remarked, "The trip to the Bob Wills Ranch takes about an hour and a half."

Joe stated, "That name sounds familiar. I think Kyle used to play his songs in the barracks."

Britta responded, "Bob Wills grew up on the ranch Kyle leases north of Turkey. He was famous for western swing. Each year there's a Bob Wills festival in Turkey. Maybe you and Megan would like to join Kyle and me at this year's festival?" Neither responded; Britta let it drop.

Megan pulled to the side of the road behind Rachel's truck. Britta exited. "I have the key. I'll close the gate behind you. It's about a mile to the Wills place." She unlocked the gate and swung it to the side, waiting as the two trucks passed. Rachel continued down a dirt road. Britta closed the gate and slid into the passenger seat. "You might want to let Rachel get ahead of us; her truck will kick up dust."

Megan sat, watching the truck's lights disappear into the dust. After the dust settled, Megan followed. The plowed field ended after they drove a half a mile; the road continued down a cedar-lined track.

Joe remarked, "Don't ask me to tell you how to get home."

The gray light in the eastern sky announced the approaching dawn. Joe opened his window; the smell of cedar overwhelmed them. "That smells great."

Britta acknowledged, "It sure does."

Megan addressed Britta. "Sorry for being so quiet but when I drive, I focus only on driving,"

Britta answered, "Maybe tonight we'll have a chance to talk."

They saw Rachel standing by an open gate. After Megan drove through, Rachel closed the gate. Britta remarked, "The working pens are up ahead."

Chapter 50

TORTILLAS AND
REFRIED BEANS

A collection of trucks and trailers sat parked next to a set of pens. Kyle walked up to Megan's truck. "I see you made it. We've got about a half-hour before we ride out." Kyle added, "Unload and saddle your horses and join us at the cook tent."

Their horses saddled and secured, Joe and Megan followed the smell of fresh-brewed coffee. She remarked, "This looks like something out of the old west."

They joined Rachel and Sue. Joe recognized the artist who painted the sign on his store. As he approached, Joe commented, "Brad, I didn't know you were a cowboy."

He remarked, "I'm not, but I know how to cook. Y'all come over to the fire and have something to eat." Sue walked over and kissed Brad on the cheek. Joe thought, *Brad's a lucky man.*

A group of riders stood drinking coffee and munching tortillas filled with refried beans. Brad handed out cups of steaming coffee and tortillas to the new arrivals.

Kyle approached. "We'll ride out at daylight. Jose will lead one group and Cowboy the other. We've decided who will be in each group."

Cowboy's group included Joe, Megan, and two cowboys. A daywork cowboy recognized Joe. "Mr. D'Angelo, nice to see you again."

Joe smiled and said, "That was some day we had gathering cows south of Palo Duro."

"You got that right. I see you've got a different horse today."

Joe looked at Megan. "This horse belongs to Ms. Warlock."

The young cowboy tipped his hat. "Nice to meet you, ma'am. That's a fine-looking mare, and that gelding you're riding is stout."

"Joe and I have been working with them. Today is their first time gathering cows."

The cowboy smiled. "That's okay. The last time I rode this horse, we had a rodeo."

His partner laughed, "By God, he rode that plug out."

Cowboy interrupted the conversation. "Time to move out." His horse started at a canter. "We're going to the end of this ranch; it should take fifteen minutes. That'll give the sun time to clear the horizon."

Joe looked back to see Jose's group disappear over a brush-covered ridge.

A wire gate and fence blocked the road. Cowboy pulled up; the group waited behind him.

He said, "We'll let the horses relax for a few minutes." His hand blocked the sun as it rose in the eastern sky. The morning chill dissipated. "We'll spread out along the fence line. The ranch ends at the river."

Cowboy looked at the young cowboys. "Y'all ride to the river. When you're in place, head to the pens. I'm going to anchor this end of the line. Joe and Megan will take the middle." He hesitated, then said, "Keep any cows you find in front of you." When he came up next to Joe, he said, "Remember all the plans we made in the service?"

Joe answered, "Yup. They're great until the first shot."

Cowboy laughed. "See you at the pens."

Kyle drove up with his feed truck. He rolled down his window. "I'm going to hit my horn, and maybe some of the cows will follow me."

Cowboy sat talking to Kyle while the others rode to their assigned places; he nodded at Kyle. "Looks like they're in place." Kyle rolled up his window and headed toward the corrals.

The sound of the truck's horn disturbed the quiet of the morning. Joe was in position, about a thousand feet from Cowboy. He pointed Daisy north and said, "Okay, girl, here we go." A light touch and the horse started at a slow walk. He could see Megan paralleling him.

Chapter 51

THORNS AND QUICKSAND

Joe watched two cows and their calves head toward the feed truck.

Megan was herding a large bull when suddenly it pivoted and charged her horse. Oscar nimbly leaped sideways.

Joe's horse ran at the bull. He yelled and swung his rope. The bull backed away, turned, and ran toward the sound of the truck's horn.

Joe asked, "Are you okay?"

Megan stroked Oscar's withers. "Thanks to Oscar, I'm fine." Then, she added, "You weren't going to rope that bull, were you?"

Joe shook his head and remarked, "These horses know what they're doing. Oscar didn't panic, and Daisy ran straight at that bull." He chuckled. "If I had roped that bull, you'd be making funeral arrangements. The critter blinked." They watched the bull disappear into the brush.

They rode through mesquite, the thorns shredding their jackets and gloved hands; Joe rode through what looked like a red clay patch. Suddenly, Daisy sank up to her belly. Megan saw the mishap and rushed to help him.

Joe petted Daisy. "Okay, girl get us out of here." Daisy slowly moved, pawing her way through to the side. As Megan arrived, Joe said, "Did you see that?"

Megan's face lit up. "You handled that perfectly."

He patted Daisy again. "She handled it."

At the pens, trucks and trailers were parked to form an alleyway. The cows followed Kyle's truck through the gate. Riders brought up the rear. After all the cows were in the corral, a rider rode to the gate, dismounted, and closed it.

Cowboy's face lit up. "Good job, y'all. It's time to take your horses to water. After they've drunk their fill, tie 'em to the fence and let 'em rest." He continued, "The other crew will need some help. Y'all need to drink some water and eat something."

Joe said to Megan, "The sun feels good."

Britta and Brad joined the group with sandwiches, Gatorade, and water. Britta beamed at them.

"We have ham and cheese or bologna." Each rider grabbed a sandwich, and Brad handed out drinks; he lingered by Sue as she ate.

Cowboy talked to the group. "Jose's crew had twice the territory to cover. So we're going to ride up on the ridge, spread out, and keep the cows heading to the pens."

The sun was overhead. Joe looked at his watch; it was almost twelve thirty. He adjusted the saddle pad and tightened the cinch.

Cowboy commented, "The ridge runs the length of the ranch."

The group followed Cowboy as the road rose before them. They crested the ridge and surveyed the territory. A windmill in the distance turned in the gentle breeze. A turkey buzzard circled.

Cowboy said, "Y'all follow me." The riders guided their sure-footed horses along the jagged ridge. At the top of a bluff, Cowboy halted. He took a pair of binoculars from his saddlebag and scanned the valley below them.

He pointed. "There they are." Joe and the others looked where he indicated. A cloud of dust moved slowly across the horizon. "They're gonna push them to the fence and turn them toward us. We've got to block any cow that wants to head back down the pasture."

The herd of cows was larger than the group Joe's crew brought in. It took half an hour for the cows to approach the ridge. The mama cows with new calves wandered from the group. Joe and Megan followed Cowboy as he slid down the hill to block the escaping cows. Cowboy and the dayworkers headed off the roaming cows; Megan and Joe's task was to push the wandering cows and calves back to the group.

The trip up the slope was treacherous; loose shale made the horses' footing unstable. Daisy and Oscar tracked the cows up and over the hill. The stragglers knew their destination, once the new arrivals saw the other cows in the pens and Kyle's feed truck. As the last of the new arrivals entered, Britta and Brad closed the gate.

The newly arrived cowboys took care of their horses. Everyone picked a spot to sit and relax.

Rachel walked over to Joe and Megan. "How was your morning?"

Joe responded, "Megan and Oscar tried to ride a bull, and I got my horse bogged down in quicksand; other than that, the ride was great."

Rachel remarked, "Some bulls don't like horses." She smiled at Megan. "I've heard you're a good rider. A lot of people would have panicked." She continued, "We have more work to do; Jose and Cowboy will tell us what to do."

Chapter 52

THE END OF A LONG DAY

Cowboy gathered the three women and Joe. "We're gonna separate the calves from their mamas. Joe and Megan will cut." He looked at Sue and Rachel. "Y'all hold the gate."

They watched Jose and the four daywork cowboys ride out of camp. Cowboy commented, "They're goin' after strays."

The penned cows had calmed down, drank water, ate hay, and nursed their calves. The riders took positions. Cowboy instructed the riders, "We'll cut the mamas out and leave the calves."

Cowboy cut out the first cow and pushed it past Rachel and Sue. Next, Joe spotted three cows standing by themselves and moved them along the fence line toward the ladies. Sue's horse sidestepped while Rachel's horse held the sorted-out cow. The cows ran past Sue and joined the other mamas. Cowboy commented, "Good cut."

Jose's crew stopped at the ridge. Two of the three cowboys went to the other section. Jose and one of the daywork cowboys headed toward the river.

Jose smiled at his partner. "No rodeo today?" Enjoying his joke, Jose laughed.

The cowboy responded. "No, sir."

Kyle drove the feed truck to the fence line and waited for the riders. Then, after letting their horses rest for a few minutes, Kyle instructed, "Let's go; we're gonna lose daylight."

Kyle led the stray cows into the pen. Jose and his riding partner headed for the ridge to wait for the other three riders. Kyle stated, "We're missing one of the men." One cowboy noted, "He went after a straggler."

The missing cowboy rode up and dismounted. Kyle asked, "You look pale. What happened?"

The young man removed his hat and wiped the sweat from the hatband. "Well, that stray turned out to be a large hog." He hesitated and continued. "I thought it would be fun to rope the pig and drag him back to camp and roast him."

After a long pause he continued, "Those hogs resent being roped. That sucker turned and charged the horse. My horse turned tail and ran. I never knew them hogs could run so fast. If you see a hog dragging a rope—leave him alone."

The assembled crowd burst into laughter.

Kyle scratching his head, asked, "Why did you rope that pig?"

The young cowboy answered, "It seemed like a good idea at the time."

Several of the group had to wipe the tears from their eyes as they doubled over with laughter.

Britta announced, "Supper will be ready in a little while. Y'all clean up!"

Britta motioned to the ladies. "Bring your towels, washcloths, and soap and come with me. We're heading to the ladies' bathing area." Then, loud enough to be heard by all, she announced, "Any man seen within a half-mile will get shot."

Kyle noted, "I think she means it."

Britta and the ladies returned after an hour. Joe said, "They're giggling like school girls."

Kyle commented, "It's a woman thing."

Brad said, "The steaks are almost ready. Time to eat."

A portable table stacked with baked potatoes, salad, and steaming steaks awaited the crew. After everyone had filled their plates, Joe and Megan found a place to sit. Pole-mounted torches complemented the light of the setting sun. Joe remarked to Megan, "You and the other women enjoyed yourselves."

Megan answered, "They're nice ladies. I'm glad you invited me."

The group sat around a campfire discussing the day's events. The daywork cowboys poked fun at the pig roper.

Joe recounted how Megan and her horse tried to ride a bull. Megan retorted, "At least I didn't try to swim in quicksand."

Kyle commented, "It's been a great day. Tomorrow we have to brand the calves and get them ready to ship. I'm going to hit the sack." The ladies retired to a large tent. The men had brought sleeping bags. Cowboy and Jose disappeared.

Kyle said to Joe and Brad, "I've swept out the horse trailer so we can spread out our sleeping bags."

Joe remarked, "This beats sleeping on the ground in Afghanistan."

"That it does."

Chapter 53

BRANDING CALVES

The rising sun and the smell of campfire coffee greeted the campers as they rolled up their sleeping bags; the women exited their tent.

Joe looked at Kyle. "Let's go get some coffee."

Britta and Brad were preparing the morning meal. Kyle greeted his wife with a hug. Britta remarked, "How was your night?"

Kyle responded, "Lonely."

The crew gathered around the coffee pot. Joe smiled at Megan and asked, "How were your accommodations?"

"Great. The girls and I talked half the night away." Then, a low rumble filled the morning air in the distance. The sound turned into a roar as two F-15s flew over the campsite at five hundred feet.

Britta looked up, "Well, I guess we're still in the twenty-first century."

Joe remarked, "Too bad."

The crew sat, enjoying their second cup of coffee. Britta stated, "Time to get started. All y'all gather firewood for the branding fires."

Jose said, "We'll have two branding stations. The day-work cowboys will switch dragging calves, and I'll work with one crew, and Cowboy will wrangle the other."

Kyle retrieved two branding irons from his truck. "We'll start as soon as the irons are hot enough."

Joe and Megan joined Cowboy, and two of the daywork cowboys gathered by the branding fire. The other group assembled near Jose. Two of the daywork cowboys mounted their horses and limbered up their ropes. Cowboy and Jose inspected the branding irons.

A nod from Cowboy started the branding, and the day-work cowboys roped the hind legs of calves and dragged them to their respective fires. Then, Cowboy and a daywork cowboy grabbed the rope, flipped the calf on its side, and pinned it to the ground.

Joe and Megan were detailed to give injections, and Kyle branded the young animal. Cowboy removed the rope. The roper returned to the calves bunched up against the fence. Both ropers maneuvered into position, with the rope loops aimed at calves. One loop missed. The successful roper yelled, "That's one."

"See how you do when the plug you're riding bucks you off." The crews laughed.

The other cowboy quickly reset his rope, caught another calf, and commented, "The day's just started." Both crews fell into a routine. If bull calves had to be castrated, it added to Kyle's and Jose's tasks.

Kyle pinched the testicle sack, sliced the top off with a flick of the wrist, and cut the spermatic cord. He tossed the severed testicles into a large bucket.

Kyle commented, "We'll have calf fries tonight."

Joe responded, "I think I'll pass."

Kyle sprayed a purple disinfectant over the wound and released the steer.

The crews worked until 11 a.m.; Kyle stood up and yelled, "Time for lunch!"

Kyle sat with Joe and Megan. "We've cut out the mamas with calves that are too young to sell." He took a drink of water and continued, "We have a problem; one of the cows, with a full bag of milk, is missing her calf."

He pointed to a solitary white-faced cow. "We have to spray the cows and load the calves. Y'all cut her from the others and push her out of the pen and follow her. We might be lucky and mama will find her baby." He suggested, "Don't follow the cow too close; let her go at her own pace."

Megan and Joe finished lunch and saddled their horses. It only took a minute to cut out the white-faced cow; she seemed eager to leave. They watched as the cow climbed the ridge road. Megan said, "I think that's enough space. Let's go."

The pair followed the cow. At the peak of the ridge, the cow cut cross-country heading for the back gate. Megan and Joe separated so that one of them always had the cow in view. Joe thought, *Mesquite and deep riverbeds don't slow her down.* The pair stayed on the cow's tail. After about a mile, she walked into a tall stand of switchgrass and mooed. Her baby jumped up and ran to her mother. The calf attacked his mother's udders.

Megan said, "That's unbelievable. That cow knew exactly where her calf was."

Joe added, "We're going to have to wait until the calf is full."

The riders watched from a safe distance as the calf drank, and the mama licked her baby.

Joe smiled and said, "I would never have believed this." Joe's horse stood next to Megan's. "I could get used to this."

Megan reached out, squeezed Joe's hand, and smiled.

The riders waited fifteen minutes; the calf moved away from the mama cow. Megan said, "Okay, let's see if we can get this pair back to the pens." The riders flanked the cow and slowly approached the pair. The cow moved, and the calf followed. It took an hour to reach the pens as the calf had to stop and rest. As they crested the ridge, the cow and calf walked to the corrals.

Kyle's feed truck stood in an empty pen. The cow and calf entered. Kyle closed the gate. "Good job, y'all might make cowboys."

Joe pointed at his shredded shirt. "I think I've qualified." The three shared a laugh.

The calves to be shipped were already loaded. The calves too small to sell stood near their mamas.

Kyle said, "Help me push the cows and calves out of the pen." Britta, Joe, and Megan moved behind the small herd. As soon as the gate opened, the animals needed little encouragement to leave.

Britta walked over and told them, "Time to head out."

Megan, Joe, and Britta spent the ride home recapping the highlights of the roundup.

Britta commented to Megan, "You and Joe work well together."

Megan smiled. Joe was red-faced.

Chapter 54

COWBOY'S HOME PLACE

One morning, Joe unlocked the store as usual. What surprised him was seeing Cowboy parked in front of the store.

Cowboy got out of his truck and walked into the store. "Howdy, Joe." He smiled. "The roundup was great."

"That it was."

"I want to talk to you about something—do you have time?"

Joe nodded. "I've got some fresh coffee in the back. I'll get two cups. How do you like it?"

Cowboy pointed to the back of his hand.

Joe laughed. "Have a seat. I'll be right back."

Cowboy took off his hat and sat in the customer chair near Joe's workbench. Joe returned with two cups of coffee and set them on his workbench.

"Joe, I've been thinking. I have a major decision to make about my family ranch south of Quitaque." Then he frowned. "I hate to say it, but I've got to retire."

"That's crazy. You're not that old."

"Well, I'm 75."

Joe thought, *I hope I look that good when I'm his age.* "That's got to be hard to think about."

"Nah. I never lie to myself. I'm getting too old, and I want to have time to visit my grandchildren." At the mention of his grandchildren, a smile filled his face. "My problem is the land is in a sacred trust passed down in my family. Fifteen cousins and second cousins own the ranch. My son is a doctor and lives in San Diego, California, and my daughter is a book editor living in Boise, Idaho. I know they're not interested in ranching. So I'm thinking about selling the place."

Joe spoke slowly. "Do you think I could visit your ranch?"

Cowboy answered, "That's what I'd like you to do; maybe we could make a deal."

"Would you mind if Megan came with us?"

"I was hoping she would."

As soon as Cowboy departed, Joe called Megan.

"I can't believe what just happened." He explained his meeting with Cowboy. Deliberately, Joe left out how Cowboy was anxious for her to come with him. They conversed for a few minutes. Megan agreed to go with Joe on the ranch visit.

It took a week to arrange everyone's schedule, and they agreed on dates for the trip. Cowboy suggested a one-day excursion.

It was a beautiful spring day when Megan and Joe set out for the ranch, horse trailer in tow. Cowboy had suggested riding horseback was the best way to see the ranch. Cowboy had given Joe directions, and they agreed to meet at the ranch gate at 10 a.m.

Joe and Megan arrived on time. Cowboy stood at the opened gate and waved them through; a metal sign above the entrance read Flat Top Mountain Ranch.

Cowboy secured the main gate and walked to the driver's window. "Follow me to the cabin." He could see the question on Joe's face. "Don't worry, your truck and horse trailer will make it. I don't have any cows on the place—no need to bother with the other gates."

Joe followed Cowboy's truck; the road led through cedar and mesquite bushes.

Megan exclaimed, "This place is beautiful; I've never seen anything like this before." The rough land was surrounded on two sides by the caprock escarpment.

The road angled down. Joe remarked, "Looks like a streambed," as they passed over a large culvert.

Megan studied the tracks in the streambed sand. "There's a lot of animal prints."

Cowboy's truck crested the top. Joe's truck labored but made it. "Whew."

Another pasture greeted them. Megan said, "This is the nicest stand of buffalo grass I've seen in West Texas." She added, "One of my game warden duties was to inventory the grasses."

They drove over another streambed; the banks were not as steep as the first one. As they passed through another gate,

Cowboy was waiting. "I guessed you'd make it. That first streambed was the test."

Joe answered, "I'm glad we passed."

"The next steep grade we have is down to the cabin. Use low gear and go slow."

"Is this another test?"

Cowboy laughed and got back in his truck.

They followed their host to an open field dotted with flowers—red, yellow, and purple on a carpet of buffalo grass. Joe and Megan alternated remarking on the beauty surrounding them.

"Wow."

"This is gorgeous!"

"Spectacular."

They ran out of superlatives as the road angled down another steep hill. Flat areas reduced the angle of descent.

Megan exclaimed, "I can't believe this place."

Joe finished her thought. "It's almost paradise."

Chapter 55

DRIPPING SPRINGS

Cowboy motioned Joe to park his rig next to a set of pens. Cowboy suggested, "Why don't you put your horses in the pens? There's plenty of grass and water."

With the horses tended to, they followed Cowboy up the steps of the covered porch. "Welcome to world headquarters of the Flat Top Mountain Ranch. It ain't fancy, but it's built stout and is self-sufficient—you're off the grid." The open floor plan had a pine table, four chairs, a plain sofa, and three reclining armchairs. The woodblock counters contained a steel sink, a four-burner gas stove, and cabinets. Off the living room was a door to the bathroom and closet. Cowboy motioned Joe and Megan to follow him. Another door off the living room led to a bedroom furnished with a cedar wood bedroom set. Megan asked, "Do you know how old the bedroom set is?"

"My grandfather told me it was old when he was young." Cowboy smiled and said, "The mattress has been upgraded a few times."

The couple followed their host to a covered back porch. Cowboy noted, "All the porches were added to the original structure." An outdoor table and four chairs sat to one side. A seating area of three chairs and side tables took up the other side. "Let's sit a minute. I need a bottle of water. How about y'all?" Megan and Joe both nodded.

They sat, drinking their water and listening to the sounds of the birds. Megan said, "I hear doves, blue jays, and cardinals."

Cowboy noted, "You have good hearing." A series of splashing sounds drew their attention. "The pond is stocked with largemouths, catfish, minnows, and perch." He continued, "Let's sit a few more minutes. Then I want to show you something special."

"How can you top this?"

"Let's take a short walk."

Joe and Megan followed Cowboy. They headed out the cabin's front door toward a large cottonwood tree; fine cottonwood fluff drifted from its leafy branches.

Cowboy said, "These cottonwoods don't last long, but they sure are great shade trees." As they passed the cottonwood, a path wove through thick undergrowth. To the left of the trail, the stream trickled toward the pond. The track opened into a grass-filled valley. Brush-covered walls rose on either side of the streambed. Joe and Megan stopped to admire the view.

Cowboy waved them on, saying, "The real show is up ahead."

The path was on high ground bordering the stream; minnows darted through the shallows. The well-worn trail rose and fell with the contours of the land. Finally, they crossed a bridge made of railroad ties and stopped at a clearing.

Cowboy motioned to the cliff across from the trail. "Look at the water dripping through the rocks. These are the dripping springs."

The course ended at a red clay and sandstone ridge. The dripping water created moss-covered stalactites. Years of erosion formed a waterfall into a pond and overflowed into the stream. The trickle of water sparkled as it made its way down the cliff.

Joe said, "I never dreamed that a place like this was possible in this part of the world."

"Most Easterners have the same reaction. Legend has it that this is where my ancestors used to bathe."

Megan exclaimed, "Sounds like a good idea." Her face turned red as the men exchanged glances. "Not now." The gentle laughter of the men brought a smile to her face.

Cowboy sat on a tree stump. Megan and Joe found a seat nearby. "Well, what do you think?"

Megan began, "You're a lucky man. I don't know why you would ever leave this place."

Cowboy smiled sadly and said, "Let's head back to the cabin."

The group relaxed on the porch. Cowboy pointed to another path next to a small windmill. "See that path? It leads to a trail down to another streambed. Why don't you two saddle up and follow me?"

They retrieved the horses from the corrals and made them ready for the ride. The riders swung into their saddles; Cowboy led the way. They circled the pond and found a path leading to another streambed.

As they exited the brush-lined route, Cowboy pulled up. "This streambed is about a mile long—just follow me." Cowboy led as Megan and Joe relaxed in their saddles and admired the scene before them.

As the trail progressed past red clay cliffs and granite rock formations, Megan said, "I don't think I have words to describe this."

Joe noted, "I've been in a few areas in this country but nothing like this."

Cowboy chuckled. "The Palo Duro Canyon's ending is just as spectacular as its beginning."

As they followed the trail, several other streambeds emptied into the main course. At a junction of three streams, Cowboy pulled up again. He swung his right leg over the saddle horn.

"This is the ranch's version of the three corners." He pointed south and said, "This leads to a large overhang—it's worth visiting but not today." Cowboy shifted and pointed at a barely visible path. "That takes you to the gate. Another amazing trip for another day." He suggested, "Let's step down and let the horses eat some grass."

Joe and Megan dismounted and loosened the cinch strap on their horses' saddles. Cowboy nodded and explained. "When my ancestors worked for Charles Goodnight, they saw him fire a cowboy for not loosening the cinch on his horse when he dismounted."

He shook his head. "My dad would chew me out for forgetting to do it. That horse doesn't want to be here—he's doing you a favor carrying your butt." He went on, "You two have already learned that lesson."

They mounted and rode another half-mile through stream-filled meadows and brush-lined paths. Cowboy urged his horse up a path that climbed out of the streambed and called out, "Relax and follow me." They followed a narrow path past an overlook and saw water cascading down a well-worn granite outcrop.

Joe was captivated. "This place is magical."

The trail ended as they passed another overhang. The ranch road greeted the riders. Cowboy walked his horse down the road to the bottom of the ravine. He dismounted and led his horse to the stream. Megan and Joe joined him. As their horses drank, Cowboy pulled bottles of water from his saddlebag.

"Let's stop for a while."

Megan and Joe held hands as their horses drank. The magic of the moment needed no words. Joe and Megan walked around, leading their horses.

Cowboy commented, "This stream comes out of the ground about a quarter-mile from here. I'm afraid we've got to get back."

The ride up the road was steep, but the horses climbed it effortlessly. Finally, the three arrived at an open pasture across from the second gate. Cowboy's horse knew the way to the cabin, and the others followed.

At the cabin, Cowboy hooked up his horse trailer and loaded his horse. Megan and Joe secured their horses in their trailer for the ride to the front gate. Cowboy remarked, "I've got to do something with this place. I want you to think about what your plans are." He paused. "I've got to be going. Lock the front gate when you leave. We'll talk some more in a few days."

Megan asked, "How can Joe and I thank you?"

Cowboy answered, "You already have." He swung his trailer and truck around and headed for the road. He waved as he disappeared up the road.

Joe's arms reached out to Megan, and he said to her, "We've got to talk about our future."

Her eyes gleaming with joy, Megan nodded and said, "Yes, we do!" as she stepped into his embrace.

Chapter 56

TWO HEARTS JOIN

Spending time with Megan was arousing feelings Joe thought were dead. The same feeling kept surfacing: *Am I dishonoring my wife's memory and the love we shared?* His work kept him busy, but his thoughts wandered, and he found himself thinking of Megan's smiling blue eyes often.

One morning, Rachel and Sue stepped into the shop. Rachel asked, "Coffee time—join us?"

"Sounds good."

He locked the door to his store, and they walked past the old courthouse. He commented, "It's a shame that courthouse isn't put to use."

Rachel answered, "Yes, that beautiful old building being empty is sad. Something with no purpose is tragic."

Joe nodded and thought, *Is she talking about me?* He responded, "Maybe someone will find a use for it."

The three friends spotted the usual suspects at the coffee shop and pulled up chairs. Joe noticed that Sue sat next to Brad and had joined hands as they drank their coffee. It was humorous watching Brad trying to heft a coffee cup with his left hand. The conversation was friendly and adjourned at ten thirty.

Joe and the ladies reached the gun repair shop. Before he entered, he asked, "Can I talk to you ladies for a moment?" Rachel and Sue nodded and followed Joe into his shop. They sat patiently, watching Joe fidget with a screwdriver, waiting for him to speak.

Finally, he looked at Sue. "We have similar reasons for moving here. I couldn't miss the affection you share with Brad."

Rachel reached out and gently removed the screwdriver from Joe's hand. "You're trying to make up your mind about your feelings for Megan?"

"What makes you think that?"

Rachel and Sue exchanged glances and almost lost their composure. Rachel smiled and said, "Don't you think we see how you and Megan act when you're together?"

Sue added, "When we women went to clean up at the roundup, the only thing Megan talked about was you."

Joe's face reddened, and a broad smile swept over his face and brightened his eyes. "I guess you've answered my question."

Sue's face lost all emotion, and she said, "Joe, we both have pasts. I've concluded that I have to live for tomorrow." She stood and motioned Joe to stand. She wrapped her arms around him. "We have new lives; it's time to let the past go."

Rachel couldn't resist. "Can I be the flower girl?"

"What?" Joe laughed, and the ladies joined him.

The time dragged until Wednesday. Megan arrived to pick him up at the usual time; Joe slid into the passenger seat. Before Megan put the truck in gear, she stated, "In two weeks, I have to open the riding stable."

Joe responded, "I guess that will end our weekly dates?"

"Why?" she asked. Their hands touched, which led to an embrace. When their lips met, Joe knew he'd found what he was searching for; the horses would have to wait. Joe slid her over toward the passenger side, opened the door, and led her into his apartment.

Their hour together changed the atmosphere between them as they drove toward Palo Duro Canyon. Joe commented, "It's just like riding a bike; you never forget how to do it."

Megan replied, "Don't act smart. I like you the way you are."

Joe answered, "Yes ma'am."

"Time to get to work."

Chapter 57

SHADOWS FROM THE PAST

The next day, Joe was at his regular table in the Night Owl Café, sipping a latte. Rowdy handed a takeout order to a customer and made his way to Joe's table. "How did the roundup go?"

"It went well."

Rowdy continued, "I've heard from my friends at the DEA that the head of a cartel has hired a hitman to take you out."

Joe's brow wrinkled. "What?"

"Those criminals who tried to hold you up got out of jail and headed back to Mexico. My sources tell me they blamed you for upsetting their plans and killing their partner."

Joe laughed. "I've arrested mafia bosses and drug dealers and been threatened by professionals."

Just then, Megan joined them. She sat next to Joe.

"Who's threatening you?"

Joe waved his hand and said, "This is nothing to worry about." Then, he collected himself. "Do we have a date for Wednesday to work the horses?"

"Sure, but I want to hear about this threat."

Rowdy explained what he had heard. Megan remarked, "This doesn't sound like nothing."

Joe stood. "I've got to get back to work." He looked at Megan with a smile and said, "I'll see you Wednesday."

Rowdy stood up. Megan said, "Please stay and help me understand what's going on."

Rowdy sat again and said, "Joe killed a cartel member in a holdup before he left New York. The group that tried to hold up Joe's shop was from that same organization, and they said their partners died because of Joe. My sources tell me the leader of the cartel is angry and wants revenge."

Megan exclaimed, "That's crazy."

Rowdy clasped his hands together with a sad smile. "The cartels have been successful because they eliminate anyone who crosses them." He slowly twirled his thumbs. "My friends at the DEA are watching the leader of the cartel. They'll find out who the assassin is."

"Isn't there any way to stop this?"

"No. The police must catch the criminals in the act."

"Why?"

Rowdy answered, "Because that's the way it is."

That night a loud knock on the door broke Joe's concentration. He laid down the book he was reading and glanced at the security monitor. *It's Jose; I wonder what he wants?* Joe opened the door.

An excited Jose said, "I need to tell you something."

Joe motioned Jose to follow him into the living quarters and pointed to a chair in the room. *Jose's never excited. What's up?*

Jose sat, and looked solemnly at Joe. "When I was in Mexico, my brother told me that the cartel is planning to kill you." He continued, "These are bad hombres; I think you should leave town."

Joe shook his head. "I appreciate the warning, but I can't leave. My business and my home are here now." He stood and grasped Jose's hand. "You're a good friend."

His eyes downcast, the Mexican cowboy left. As he walked to his truck, he looked up at the sky and muttered, "Watch over him."

Chapter 58

THE ASSASSIN

Juarez, Chihuahua, Mexico

Macho had dealt with Pablo and his cartel before. The guards knew him and stood aside as he entered the compound.

Macho stood in the doorway to the drug lord's office. Pablo motioned him to a chair. "I have a job for you."

Macho's cold eyes appraised Pablo. "I need to know the assignment before I agree."

"We've been trying to expand into new territory. Unfortunately, a retired New York cop is getting in our way."

"Killing cops is not good for business."

"I'll make it worth your while."

Macho thought, *Maybe I'll retire with the money I'll make.* "How much will you pay?"

"Because it's in the U.S., I'll pay you more than your normal rate."

"Explain the details."

Pablo told Macho the target's name and address and that Joe D'Angelo had killed his brother in New York and one of his men in Canyon, Texas. Next, he showed Macho a photograph of Joe. Macho examined the picture. "I have to think about this."

"When can I expect an answer?"

"Within a week."

Macho left the compound and drove until he was out of sight. On a quiet street, he scanned his car for tracking devices. The first one was easy to find. He knew the second one would be well concealed. His scanner continued to beep. The second device was a new design and hidden behind a hub cap. He thought, *We play this game every time I meet with Pablo.*

He murmured, "Let's see if you like following a garbage truck."

It took Macho an hour to find a parked garbage truck. The sanitation workers were at lunch in a nearby cantina. He inserted the tracking unit under the floorboard on the driver's side. He chuckled as he drove away.

Macho planned every detail of the hit—he took no chances. However, he needed to do more work and what Pablo never knew was that he didn't work alone.

Google Maps had a picture of D'Angelo's shop. The site on the square in Canyon, Texas, offered many shooting locations. A little research revealed an abandoned courthouse across the street from D'Angelo's shop.

Macho's advance men spent two days in Canyon and returned with the information he'd requested.

The advance men didn't notice the curtains move in the small house across the street when they checked out the courthouse. The lead DEA agent commented, "It looks like Macho is getting ready for another visit."

Macho's men also stopped in Del Rio, Texas, to see a local arms dealer. The dealer had no idea who they represented and didn't care. The Remington 700 hunting rifle's price was five thousand dollars and included two boxes of .308 cartridges. In addition, the dealer guaranteed that the serial number had been obliterated. The cash price included a stand and a Crossfire II scope.

One of the advance men gave the dealer a key to a locker in the bus station with instructions to wait until he received word to deliver the rifle.

The advance man paid half up front and would pay the balance after the dealer delivered the rifle. The dealer knew what happened to people who double-crossed an assassin.

★ ★ ★

As promised, Macho kept his appointment with Pablo. Pablo asked, "Will you accept the assignment?"

"Yes. It will cost one million dollars."

"Too much. I'll pay five hundred thousand."

Macho stood and turned toward the door.

Pablo stood. "Wait, I'll pay seven hundred and fifty thousand dollars."

Macho turned and nodded. "Half now and the balance when the job is complete."

"When will you complete the assignment?"

"In two weeks."

Neither man extended their hand. They knew the deal—no need to shake hands.

Chapter 59

MACHO HEADS NORTH

The border guard smiled as he waved a car through the checkpoint and said, "Enjoy your visit to the United States." The Border Patrol agent thought, *That was the easiest five thousand dollars I've ever made.*

Macho drove to the Del Rio bus stop and circled the street, checking for a tail. None apparent, he entered the long-term lot, turned off the ignition, got out, and locked the door. His crew had parked the car he'd use for the assignment two rows down.

Macho walked into the bus station waiting room and sat for thirty minutes, pretending to read a newspaper. Finally, he stood and walked around, looking in store windows. The coffee shop smelled of fresh cinnamon buns. *It's good the gringos don't allow smoking.* An empty table at the far wall gave him a perfect view of the entrance and the other customers.

A waitress with a soiled apron, flaming red hair, and a large bust sauntered over to Macho's table and asked, "What can I get you?"

"Café negro, por favor."

She rested her hand on her overlarge hip and stated, "I guess you want black coffee?"

"Si."

Five minutes later, the waitress returned with a cup of coffee and a check. "Pay this on your way out." She put the coffee in front of him and the bill on the table. She turned and sashayed back to the counter.

"Gracias."

Without turning, she answered, "Whatever."

He went to the locker, picked up the package, and walked out of the bus station, looking for his next ride. Macho's crew had stolen a 1985 Chevrolet Nova and replaced the license plates; a mechanic had installed a new, more powerful engine and extra-wide tires. It was parked on the street around the corner from the bus station. Macho started the engine, turned on his new smartphone, and asked Google for directions to Canyon, Texas.

DEA agents sitting in a nondescript van contacted the operations center. The senior agent commented, "Looks like we put the tracking device in the correct vehicle." He called the operations center. "You can retrieve the drone."

"Roger that. If you need any further assistance, contact us."

The agent looked at the screen showing the location of the tracking device. "He's headed north."

The senior agent said, "We can stay two miles back. Let's see where he's going." He mused, "We'd never catch him in a race."

The sun reflected off the white sands of the missile range. The agent asked, "Would you look in my bag and see if you can find my sunglasses?"

The senior agent retrieved two pairs of sunglasses. "Here's your glasses. Better fall back another mile in this flat country."

The drive was pleasant. Macho enjoyed driving on an empty road in the Chihuahua Desert. He thought, *Let's see what this heap can do.* He jammed the gas pedal to the floor. The car's speed jumped from sixty-five miles an hour to one hundred in under three seconds. Macho cruised for three miles at a blistering pace.

The junior agent exclaimed, "Look at the speed."

The senior agent remarked, "He's testing the car. Set your speed to catch up gradually. As long as we have a satellite connection, we'll know where he is."

Route 54 divided the city of Alamogordo, New Mexico. Macho spent a half-hour winding his way through the town and stopped in a convenience store parking lot for another half hour. The agents rolled into town and quickly found him but stayed well out of sight. The DEA agents parked in a roadside rest area and waited.

Finally, the driver put the car in gear. "He's on the move."

His partner cautioned, "Let's watch for a while."

Macho checked his rearview mirror. *I must be getting old. I can't shake the feeling that I'm being followed.* He headed north and turned off at Route 70, and headed toward Ruidoso. The scenery changed as he entered Lincoln National Forest, then drove past a sign: *Welcome to the Apache Reservation*. Pinyon pines, juniper, and spruce dotted the landscape as the elevation increased. In the distance, a snow-covered mountain peak stood guard over the land.

Macho knew of a motel that took cash and asked no questions. The front desk had a sign: *Ring the bell for service*. It took three rings to get a sleepy Hispanic man to open a door behind the desk. "How can I help you?"

"A single room for one night."

"Credit card or cash?"

"Cash."

"Forty-three dollars."

No further conversation was necessary. Macho paid, and the clerk handed him a key and disappeared into the back. Macho carried his overnight bag and the package he had picked up at the bus station into the room. He dropped his bag and opened the box containing the sniper rifle. Macho also found a cleaning kit with solvents and patches. His hands had muscle memory and wasted no motion as he disassembled and cleaned the weapon.

Next, Macho removed a photograph of Joe D'Angelo from a manila envelope and a drawing of Canyon's courthouse square with measured distances to the gunsmith's store from various angles.

Macho's pursuers drove past his motel and headed toward Roswell, New Mexico. They got a room in a motel across the road from the race track. The agents agreed on a watch schedule. One agent slept, and the other read a book and kept his eye on the tracking device's screen.

At 4 a.m., a man rapped on Macho's motel room door. Macho gave him the keys to the Nova. "Drive through Roswell and set the GPS toward DFW airport. Dump this car in the DFW long-term parking lot, and pick up the car you parked there last week. Meet me in Amarillo at the Budget Motel." He mused *I hope the DEA agents enjoy their trip.* Macho waited two hours and headed east. *Next stop, Amarillo.*

The senior agent shook his companion. "The target's moving."

"Which way is he headed?"

"Toward Roswell. We have time to clean up and let him get ahead of us."

Chapter 60

OPENING THE RIDING STABLE

Canyon, Texas

On the last Wednesday before opening day, Joe and Megan stood in front of the riding stable's main corral. Joe asked, "What do you want me to do?"

Megan said, "The horses need grooming."

Joe attached a lead rope to Oscar's halter, tied the rope to a pipe fence, and brushed him. The dark winter hair fell away. A light tan undercoat transformed the horse's looks. Speckles of black appeared and contrasted with his tail and mane. Joe stood back. "Never realized you were so beautiful."

Megan exited the cabin and stood by Joe. "He's a beauty." She smiled at Joe. "Seven horses to go."

Joe laughed. "I expect a good reward."

"Sir, that sounds lecherous."

"You catch on fast."

The day ended as the sun set on the western ridge of the canyon. An orange glow turned the walls of the eastern escarpment into a striped riot of color. Megan and Joe sat on the porch, admiring the spectacle. The meandering stream was glistening in the fading light. Megan's face shone. "We've had a good day."

The following day, Joe followed his usual routine of weight training followed by a three-mile run. His repair work was backing up. He thought, *Yesterday was fun, but I've committed to my customers.* As he ran, he planned his workday.

Despite his commitment to his customers, thoughts of Megan crowded into his mind.

As he stepped into his workspace in the front of the store, he said out loud, "Time to get busy."

Joe liked to work on firearms. Soon he blocked out everything else and concentrated on the repair. At 10 a.m., Sue and Rachel stopped to ask him to join them for coffee. Joe shook his head.

"Thank you for the invite, but my work is backing up."

Rachel said, "We'll bring you coffee. Have you eaten anything today?"

Joe answered, "Could you have Juan make me a breakfast burrito?"

"My pleasure."

By ten thirty, the women returned with Joe's coffee and burrito. Rachel placed the food on the counter. Joe joined Rachel and Sue. "You're a lifesaver, thank you."

Rachel beamed. "We have some news."

The women waited as Joe unwrapped his breakfast and opened his coffee. Joe looked up. "Well, what's the news?"

"Sue and Brad are going to get married."

"That's great. Maybe I can be the flower boy or ring bearer."

Sue laughed and Rachel continued, "We could plan a double wedding. How about it?"

Joe's hands trembled slightly. He put the burrito down. "I don't know about that."

Sue's elbow jabbed Rachel's ribs, and Rachel's smile vanished.

Sue continued, "Don't get her wrong. She's a romantic and loves to kid around."

"You ladies are good friends. Things are going well with Megan and me, but we both have histories and haven't discussed it."

Sue held Joe's hand and said, "Take your time; we're always available if you need to talk."

"That means a lot to me." He looked at Rachel. "How much money do I owe you?"

"On the house."

Rachel and Sue headed for their store.

Sue remarked, "Joe's troubled." Then she shook her head. "Did you see Joe's hands shake?"

Rachel responded, "A lot of military vets have issues they don't discuss. Maybe I should keep my big mouth shut." She sighed.

"Good idea."

Chapter 61

WEDDING BELLS

Scattered clouds drifted across a light blue sky as Brad walked into Joe's store. Joe greeted him, "How's your day going?"

Brad shifted his weight to avoid Joe's gaze.

"What's the matter?"

"I have to ask you a favor."

"Just ask it."

Brad placed his hands on the counter and looked at his hands. "Rachel said you and I are alike. I don't see it, but I know we both don't make friends too easy."

"You got that right."

"Sue and I are going to be married next Saturday, and I'd like you to be my best man."

"I'd be honored."

Brad's shoulders relaxed like the weight of the world was lifted off him. A broad smile spread across his face. "Rachel wanted to make a big shindig out of our wedding, but Sue and I want a private wedding."

Joe came around the counter and pulled Brad toward him with a manly hug. "Just tell me the time and place."

"Ten o'clock this Saturday at the Methodist Church."

The wedding party consisted of Kyle, Rachel, Joe, and the bride and groom. Brad fidgeted as he waited for Sue. Then, people started entering the church.

Brad looked at Rachel. "I thought this was going to be a small wedding?"

Rachel said, "It is, but the church is a public building." With a passive face, she continued, "You don't realize it, but people are here because they care about you. Relax."

The church pianist began playing "Here comes the Bride." All eyes shifted to the rear of the church. Sue tentatively stepped forward. Kyle gently placed her hand on his bent arm and took the first step—Sue gripped his arm and moved with him. Kyle nodded toward Brad. Joe stood quietly next to Brad. As Brad's and Sue's eyes met, tension drained from their faces.

Brad's gaze stayed on Sue, who was dressed in a cream-colored floor-length dress, and wore a diamond heart necklace below the ridge of her keyhole neckline and a crown of flowers on her head. Brad whispered to Joe, "I think my heart skipped a beat."

Kyle ushered the newly married couple into the fellowship hall. A punch bowl and a wedding cake sat on a white lace table cloth sprinkled with flower petals. Rachel guided Brad and Sue to a spot near the entrance. Well-wishers hugged and shook the hands of the new couple. Rachel hugged Brad, stepped back, took his right hand, and turned it face down, exposing his knuckles.

Brad exclaimed, "What?"

Rachel answered, "Just checking."

Sue swatted Rachel lightly with her wedding bouquet.

Next to the couple was a table covered with gifts. Sue saw a ceramic pot with a rose painted on it and a card saying, "Best Wishes, Aunt May." She began laughing. Rachel turned to see what Sue was looking at, and their laughter filled the hall.

Megan was seated at a decorated table with Joe, sipping punch and eating a piece of wedding cake. Joe pointed out the subject of the laughter and the story behind it. Joe remarked, "Sue and Brad look good together."

Rachel approached them. "Joe was supposed to be the flower boy."

Megan chuckled, "Maybe next time?"

Joe's frown disappeared and was replaced by a smile. "I hope you two are enjoying yourselves!"

Chapter 62

THE WARNING

Joe had just finished cleaning a Browning Cynergy Max-5 12 gauge over-under shotgun. The burnt bronze steel finish glowed in the afternoon sun. He placed the repaired shotgun in his gun safe and texted the customer that his weapon was ready.

Joe looked at his clock. "It's three in the afternoon; no wonder my stomach's growling. Joe, you've got to stop talking to yourself." He chuckled at his joke. "Let's go to the Night Owl."

He entered the café and was greeted by Rowdy. "What can I get for you?"

"A BLT and a chai latte."

Rowdy prepared Joe's order. The café was empty. Rowdy sat across from Joe while he ate and said, "My friends at the DEA told me it's for sure. There's an assassin coming after you."

Rowdy crossed his arms and leaned on the table. "The assassin gave them the slip. They followed the car to the DFW parking lot and found the car they'd been tracking abandoned in the long-term parking."

"Is the DEA certain the assassin is coming here?"

"Their double agent heard Pablo make a deal with Macho."

"Who?"

"The assassin goes by the name Macho. No one knows his real name." Rowdy paused. "One thing the agent said is puzzling; the assassin's fee is to be paid in small denominations in U.S. currency after he kills you."

Joe responded, "Interesting."

Joe walked into the Community Bank and approached the first desk he found. "Good afternoon. I'd like to speak to Mr. Fulbright."

The dark-haired receptionist asked, "Who should I say is calling?"

"Joseph D'Angelo."

As soon as she hung up, Fulbright opened his office door. He looked at Joe. His pale face answered the question Joe had come to ask. "How can I help you?"

"I'd like to talk to you about opening a checking account."

Fulbright's hand shook as he pointed to a young woman at the next desk. "Mrs. Jones can help you." He turned, rushed back into his office, and closed the door.

Joe commented to the receptionist, "Mr. Fulbright seems busy."

The young lady smiled and shrugged her shoulders. "I just started working here."

"Thank you for your time." Joe turned and exited the bank.

Fulbright waited fifteen minutes and opened his door. "Did Mr. D'Angelo open an account?"

"No. He never talked to Mrs. Jones."

Fulbright retreated to his office and thought, *What was he doing here? Maybe I should call Pablo. But no, what can I tell him?* He knew Pablo would take care of D'Angelo. His job was to pay Macho, the assassin he'd never met.

Macho's two assistants checked into the Budget Motel and paid cash for a week's stay. Macho ushered them into his room. The men sat on the bed. "We've got to go over the plan. I need you two to go to Canyon and get into the abandoned courthouse."

They spent the next hour going over the details of the plan. "Get some rest; tomorrow is going to be a long day."

The two men retreated to their room. One spoke quietly, "I don't know how we can do this without being caught."

His companion responded, "Better to get caught than fail Macho."

Chapter 63

A VISIT FROM THE DEA

Rowdy joined Joe after he prepared his lunch. "I've arranged a meeting with the DEA agents on this case."

Joe reacted with surprise. "I didn't know this was a case."

Rowdy laughed. "I thought you were a former cop?"

"I am, but I've put that behind me."

"Joe, you've got to focus. These warnings are real, and the lead agent and his partner need to meet with you."

"Okay, when and where?"

"Tonight, my house at 7 p.m."

In his shop that afternoon, Joe looked at the gun he held in his hands. He hadn't seen many Mouser 98s. The German army used them during World War Two. With a scope mount, it was accurate. Unfortunately, the rifle had a damaged firing pin. He wasn't sure how to repair it. After assessing the needed repairs, he contacted a supply house. The conversation with the salesman turned into a discussion of the rifle's history; it was fascinating. The talk concluded with an order for a new bolt action and firing pin.

Joe called to update the customer and asked how he acquired the firearm. The customer's father had served during World War Two and had taken it from a prisoner. Joe told the customer when he expected to complete the repair. When he hung up the phone, it was six thirty. Time to go to his meeting, but he would have preferred to keep working.

Joe knocked on the door, and Mrs. Milstead opened it. "Hi, Joe, nice to see you again. Rowdy and two gentlemen are in the living room." She frowned. "I know that agent from Rowdy's time at the DEA. He called me when Rowdy was blinded."

She walked with Joe to the living room and said she'd be upstairs if they needed anything. She thought, *I don't like this.*

Rowdy stood as Joe entered the living room, as did the other two men. "Joe, meet Special Agents Art Grimstad and Lupe Alfaro."

Everyone sat and Grimstad said, "We've been working on this case for two years. A little background: after Joaquin 'El Chapo' Guzman was extradited to the U.S., the other cartels waged war to determine who would inherit his drug distribution network. The war was bad for business. The warring factions negotiated a peace treaty, and the other cartels divided up El Chapo's territory. Pablo Jimenez got the southwest. Another cartel got the northeast."

Grimstad looked at Joe. "That's where you come in. First, you killed Pablo's brother in New York, then you show up in

Canyon, and one of his men gets killed and two arrested. He knows your name—you've made an enemy."

Joe's hands formed a steeple as he thought. He asked, "Weren't the two holdup men sent back to Mexico?"

Alfaro answered, "That's correct. The DEA turned the two over to Mexican police at the border. Their bodies were found in a ditch the next day." He frowned and said, "But that's not the problem. Pablo has hired an assassin to kill you."

"This sounds like the New York Mafia."

"I've heard that Pablo's favorite movie is *The Godfather*."

Joe chuckled. "Which part?"

"Joe, this is serious." The agents described the assassin and how he slipped their surveillance. A discussion of how much money the killer would receive brought a response from Joe. "Tell him I'll take the cash."

Agent Grimstad threw up his hands. "What will it take to get your attention?"

Joe's face flushed as he said, "It's just my way of dealing with problems."

Grimstad continued, "You're a retired cop and a veteran. I know you didn't intend to start this war, but we're here to tell you that whether you like it or not, you're in the middle of this." He folded his arms and said, "We want to trap the assassin in the act and shut down the cartel's operation in this area." Then, stone-faced, he looked at Joe. "Are you in?"

Joe asked, "What can you tell me about the assassin?" Grimstad started describing Macho's background. Joe held up his hands, stopping the DEA agent's monologue. "I need to know what weapons he uses and how he carries out the hit." Grimstad's information on the details of Macho's methods was comprehensive, precisely what Joe needed to know.

Finally, Grimstad stated, "Now we've got to come up with a plan. One that doesn't get you killed."

Joe couldn't resist saying, "I've got a better idea. Convince our citizens to stop taking drugs."

Grimstad looked ready to punch something. "I wish. But here's what I think we can do . . . "

Macho slipped into the back door of the abandoned courthouse. His men had picked the lock. They had selected a window that provided the clearest view of the front of the gunsmith's shop. He got set up, and at 3 p.m, he watched Joe exit the shop. He thought, *Right on time. I've been waiting for you, gringo.*

Joe saw what he expected across the street and spoke into his hidden microphone to Agent Grimstad, with his back still to the courthouse as he locked the door. "Third floor, second window."

"Roger that." Grimstad was in place, weapon drawn.

Joe still stood at the front door, fumbling with his keys.

Macho's target was perfect—dead center in the back. Macho breathed out and squeezed the trigger.

As Joe ducked, a glancing shot drove Joe against the door. As he slumped to the ground, Agent Grimstad placed his revolver behind the assassin's ear. "Drop it, Macho."

At the sound of the gunshot, Sue and Rachel rushed out of their store. Rachel screamed, "Joe's been shot." She ran back inside the store and dialed 911, pulling Sue with her. She told the operator that Joe D'Angelo had been shot and needed an ambulance. As she disconnected the phone, she said breathlessly, "I hope they don't need a hearse. We've got to call Megan and Kyle."

A call went out through the police network. "Shots fired in Canyon's square."

Deputy Matt Williams responded, "On my way."

The ambulance and Matt arrived simultaneously. The EMTs rushed Joe onto a stretcher and headed to the ambulance while Matt cleared the scene—no sign of a shooter; he missed the broken-out window on the third floor of the courthouse across the street.

Matt yelled, "I'm coming with you." He jumped in and slammed the door; the wail of the ambulance echoed through Canyon. Matt sat next to Joe and said, "Oh God."

Joe opened his eyes and asked, "Will I do?"

Matt shook his head in disbelief. "I thought someone shot you!"

"Yes, but I'm wearing a bulletproof vest. The bullet grazed the side of the vest." He showed Matt the vest under his shirt. "The shooting was a DEA setup."

Joe removed the blanket and sat up. "Give me a hand getting this thing off."

Matt looked at Joe's side. "You're going to have a hell of a bruise."

The medic moved closer. "You need to have an X-ray."

Joe looked at Matt and said, "You need to play along. They're going to wheel me into the hospital covered by this blanket. The press must think I'm dead." He paused and continued, "The DEA has more work to do."

Megan arrived at the hospital and rushed through the lobby, where Kyle, Sue, and Rachel were at the desk. Megan asked, "What happened?"

Kyle looked down. "No one will talk to us about Joe."

Chapter 64

THE TRAP

Agent Grimstad looked in the perpetrator's eyes. "Pay attention."

Macho held up his hands. "No hablo ingles."

Grimstad pointed to the agent next to him. "This is Special Agent Alfaro—he habla—You comprendo?"

Macho smiled and said, "Okay, let's talk in English. Your Spanish is terrible."

Grimstad shook his head and continued, "You have a choice. Cooperate or be escorted to the border." He smirked, "I bet Pablo will be glad to see you when he finds out D'Angelo is alive."

"I saw the bullet strike his back and a red spot."

"That's what we wanted you to see."

Fulbright sat in his office watching the local news. Tim Tune, the local news anchor, read the monitor.

"We've received word that there has been a shooting in Canyon. Witnesses at the scene reported hearing a shot and what appeared to be a body loaded into an ambulance. At the scene is our own Christy Williams. Christy, what can you tell us?"

"Tim, the police fear that Joseph D'Angelo, a local resident, is dead. They said that the gunman disappeared. They may have a description of the getaway vehicle, but the reports are confusing."

It had been three hours since the news broadcast. Fulbright was startled when his throwaway cell phone buzzed. "Hello?"

"You know who this is?"

Fulbright responded, "If you know this number, it must be Macho."

"Correct. Listen carefully. I'll tell you where to bring the money."

His secretary knocked on his door. "Mr. Fulbright, is there anything you need? It's almost closing time."

Fulbright shook his head and, without looking up, said, "No!"

She waited for a few seconds. Finally, Fulbright said, "Goodnight." The secretary closed the door, locked her desk, and walked out of the bank. She thought, *He's a strange duck, but the money's good.* It was difficult to understand how the bank made money. There were few customers.

Fulbright walked to the treasurer's office. "Did you get the cash I need?"

"Yes, sir. Is there anything else?"

"Did you count it, and are the denominations as I requested?"

"Yes, sir." He handed Fulbright the briefcase.

Fulbright's hands trembled as he knocked on the motel room door. The rough-looking Hispanic that opened the door scanned the visitor with cold eyes. "Are you Pablo's banker?"

His sweating hands almost lost grip on the briefcase. "Yes." His eyes darted around the room. "Here is the money."

"Come in while I count it." The man took the briefcase from Fulbright.

"I can guarantee it's all there."

A smile creased the man's face. As he spoke, he pulled out his badge. "Good. You're under arrest for attempted murder and money laundering. I'm Special Agent Alfaro."

Fulbright turned to run. Agent Grimstad blocked his exit from outside the room and pointed his pistol at the banker's nose.

"Place your hands over your head." He turned to another agent who appeared. "Take him to our Amarillo office. Put him in an interrogation room." The agent handcuffed Fulbright. Grimstad pulled the agent aside. "Let him sweat. I've got to visit D'Angelo."

Chapter 65

AGENT GRIMSTAD

Canyon, Texas

Agent Grimstad walked into the hospital foyer. He approached a group of people in the waiting area. He asked, "Are any of you waiting to find out what happened to Joe D'Angelo?" The group surrounded him.

Kyle spoke, "We're all waiting. What can you tell us?"

"I'm a Special Agent for the DEA. I see Rowdy is with you. I'm going to check on D'Angelo. Rowdy can fill you in on what's been happening. Have a seat; I'll be back."

Rowdy was holding Megan's arm. He addressed the group. "Why don't we sit down? I'll tell you all I know."

Grimstad approached Deputy Williams. "I'm Special Agent Grimstad with the DEA. How's the patient?"

Williams scrutinized Grimstad and said, "Let me see some ID." The deputy scanned the DEA badge and ID. "I almost had to handcuff him to keep him in the room."

"Good job. The operation was a success. There's a crowd of people hanging around the waiting room. Is it okay if he has visitors?"

As they spoke, a doctor approached and addressed the group. "D'Angelo will be fine. He has cracked ribs and deep bruising. He'll be sore for a while, and I want to keep him in the hospital for a few days."

"Can he have company?"

"Yes, but limited to two people." Williams nodded and went to tell the group waiting outside.

The crowd gathered outside Joe's room. Megan and Kyle walked into the hospital room. Megan asked, "What happened?"

Joe smiled. "Just a little bang. Sore back, but nothing else."

"Nothing else!" Megan's eyes narrowed. "Couldn't you have told me at least something about this? I thought you were dead! We talked about a life together. I don't see how that's possible."

Joe's face reddened, and he looked down.

Kyle stepped between them. "Hey, let's calm down. Joe, tell us what happened." He looked again at Joe. "Are you ready to talk?"

"Not here, not now."

Kyle spoke, "There's a lot of people outside who want to see you. At least we know you're okay—that's what's most important. So Megan and I will head out and save this discussion for a later date."

Megan walked out of the room and took Rowdy's arm. "We have to talk." Rowdy didn't resist her gentle pressure on his arm. They headed for the reception area and sat in a secluded spot.

Megan pleaded, "Tell me what happened. I know you were with the DEA. The agent who talked to us introduced himself as a special agent."

"Nothing that happened was Joe's fault. A drug cartel was trying to set up a distribution network in the Canyon area. The DEA has been keeping an eye on this cartel and found out the head of the cartel wanted Joe killed. You already knew this part."

Rowdy reached his hand toward Megan, and she clasped his. As they held hands, he continued, "That's the way the cartels react to anyone they think is getting in their way. Joe agreed to help the agents trap the assassin in the act—it was risky, but he agreed. With information from the person the DEA has on the inside of the cartel, this operation will give the DEA enough evidence to press charges. Then, they can have the head of the cartel brought to the U.S., tried for his crimes, and sent to a maximum-security prison. It's the first step in dismantling the cartel."

Megan sat back with a grim expression on her face. "He could have so easily been killed."

Special Agent Grimstad sat in front of Fulbright. He spent a few minutes reading Fulbright's statement. The banker's eyes darted around the room, and he slowly wrung his sweaty hands.

Grimstad's eyes focused on the prisoner. "Is this all the accounts you know about?"

Fulbright looked at the ceiling. "Yes."

"What do you think Pablo will do to you after we clean out all his bank accounts?"

"My life won't be worth two cents."

Grimstad continued, "If this information is correct and you agree to testify against Pablo, we can offer you witness protection. A new identity and an out-of-the-way place to live."

"What about my family?"

"We're picking them up as we speak; they'll be waiting for you."

Border Patrol agents escorted Macho to the Mexican border. The agents nodded at the Mexican police waiting for Macho. The DEA agent accompanying Macho said, "Enjoy the rest of your life."

In handcuffs and leg manacles, Macho shuffled toward a black SUV with tinted windows.

Chapter 66

NO MORE SECRETS

Megan watched Joe's well-wishers say goodbye, and then she entered Joe's room. He was sitting on the side of the bed, trying to put on his pants.

"Where do you think you're going?"

He looked up at her. "Home."

"I've talked to your doctor. You're supposed to stay for observation."

"Why?"

"Take off your shirt. Now, give me your hand and stand up."

Joe winced as she led him to a large mirror. He faced the mirror. "Some shape. No wonder you find me irresistible."

Megan picked up a large mirror lying on the table. "Turn your back to the mirror." She handed the mirror to Joe so he could see his back. Megan smiled and placed her hand on his back, and exerted gentle pressure.

Joe winced as his body recoiled. "Ouch!"

She removed her hand and said, "That's why you have to stay here. The doctor wants to see if there is more internal damage. Stop being brave and listen." She guided Joe to the bed. Her face lost all expression. "You knew this was going to happen, and you didn't tell me."

He looked away. "I didn't . . . "

Megan cut him off. "Listen." She moved the side chair and faced him. "I thought we were making progress and building a future together."

Joe's eyes were downcast. "That's what I thought, too."

Megan smiled gently. "If we're going to move ahead—no more secrets."

Joe grasped her hand. "I promise." He drew her toward him and winced in pain.

Megan hugged him carefully and stroked his hair. Joe commented, "I didn't know I was beginning to have a bald spot."

"See, you're not perfect."

Joe feigned horror. "Really?"

Joe endured his stay in the hospital. Megan visited every day. The prognosis was that the cracks in his two ribs would mend if he refrained from strenuous exercise.

Kyle visited him on the second day. "What happened?"

Joe explained how they trapped the assassin and captured him.

Kyle frowned and said, "Sometimes you're as smart as a sack of rocks. Do you have a death wish?" Their eyes met. "What if he decided to do a head shot instead of a body shot? Not too hard at that range. That was pretty stupid."

Joe answered, "I knew the assassin's M.O."

"Just like you knew the M.O. of the sniper that almost killed you and got Willy shot."

"Pretty stupid, I guess."

"Yep."

Chapter 67

TEXAS – THE SHOW

Canyon, Texas

It felt good to be back in his shop. Working on firearms was relaxing. During one of Joe's morning visits to the Night Owl Café, Rowdy joined him. The café was empty.

"The DEA arrested all of the local dealers the banker knew of and confiscated nearly one hundred and fifty million dollars in Pablo Jimenez's bank accounts."

"Jason Fulbright's life isn't worth a nickel." Joe took a sip of his latte.

Rowdy responded, "Fulbright got off easy; he's going into the Witness Protection Program." Rowdy laced his fingers; as his thumbs tapped, he said, "The assassin's name is Macho; no one knows his real name. He refused to talk. The DEA sent his photo and fingerprints to the Mexican police—no answer."

"I thought the Mexican police cooperated with us?"

"On low-level criminals, they do. Pablo is well connected." Rowdy continued, "Macho was released at the border.

Rumor has it that Macho killed Pablo to save himself. All the DEA could find out was that Macho disappeared."

Joe sighed. "That means there'll be a new cartel selling drugs."

Megan joined the two friends. "Are you two plotting another drug bust?"

Rowdy and Joe answered as one. "No!"

Joe and Rowdy filled in Megan on the DEA's actions. She mused, "Now all they have to do is convince our people to stop taking drugs."

Joe's brow knit. "Yeah, but it'll never happen."

Megan addressed the men. "No more playing cops and robbers!"

Joe answered, "Yes." And Rowdy nodded.

Megan smiled. "We have more important issues." Her face lit up. "The show *Texas* is opening up in Palo Duro. There's a crew of our friends going to opening night. I've purchased tickets for the three of us plus your mother, Rowdy."

Rowdy said with a smile, "Then I guess we're going."

On his way to Megan's stable, Joe had passed the *Texas* show amphitheater, so he knew where it was but didn't know what to expect. The night of the show, Megan picked him up with her extended-cab pickup. Rowdy and his mother were in the back seat. Joe greeted his fellow passengers. "I never heard of this show. The only show about a state I know of is *Oklahoma*."

Mrs. Milstead commented, "I would suggest you don't say that again." Everyone chuckled.

The parking lot had disability parking; Megan had borrowed Mrs. Milstead's windshield pass. "Perfect timing. The Chuck Wagon Barbecue is opening." The foursome headed for the covered pavilion. Rowdy held his mother's arm and used his free hand to guide his white cane as it swept left to right. Megan presented their tickets and commented, "It looks like Kyle has found a spot for our crew." A guide asked Rowdy, "Is it okay if I assist you?" Mrs. Milstead, Megan, and Joe followed in her wake.

Kyle stood and greeted the group. "Have any of you ever been to a performance of this before?" All shook their heads. "That's great! You're in for a treat." The large table filled up with their friends.

Joe remarked, "I thought the show was called *Brooklyn?*"

Troy Hammond retorted, "Y'all are Texan now." The table rocked with laughter.

Kyle led the way into the theater. The group of friends occupied one row of seats in the amphitheater. Joe sat next to Kyle and looked at the empty seat next to him. "Where's Britta?"

"She'll be here directly."

The sun dropped from the sky. A spotlight illuminated a lone horseman holding a Texas flag at the top of the six hundred foot escarpment and spurred the horse into a run. Once the music started, the theater stage lights revealed the cast of the show. Kyle whispered to his friend and pointed to the rider, "There's Britta."

Joe whispered to Megan, "The rider's Britta."

"Wow."

The fifteen hundred members of the audience yelled their approval. The plot of the show revolved around a settler and the daughter of a rancher. The storyline covered the early pilgrims settling the Texas west and moving the Indigenous Comanches off their land.

Britta joined them at intermission. Joe asked, "Are these professional actors?"

"No. Most of the actors are students at West Texas A&M in Canyon."

"That was an impressive ride!"

"There are several of us who rotate the opening. It's a lot of fun."

The show ended with the chords from Beethoven's ninth symphony, fourth movement, "Ode to Joy," and a fireworks display. Finally, the group bid farewell to their friends and headed to their cars.

Joe slipped into the passenger seat; they talked about the show and the beautiful natural terrain. Megan drove to the

Milsteads' house, and they said their goodbyes to Rowdy and Mrs. Milstead.

As Joe exited Megan's truck at his door, she said, "We need to talk!"

Joe answered, "Agreed."

Chapter 68

WHAT'S NEXT?

On Saturday morning, Joe drove to the riding stable. Megan waved as he drove up; she was busy grooming a horse.

Joe asked, "Can I help?"

"Yup."

It was early, and no customers had arrived. Joe helped Megan and her hired hand saddle the horses. At 10 a.m., a young couple arrived. Megan had them sign a liability release form and they paid for an hour ride. Megan asked them, "Have you ridden before?"

The young man answered, "No. But we'd like to learn."

Joe stated, "You're from up north."

"Yes."

Joe smiled. "So am I."

Megan asked, "Joe, why don't you get them acquainted with the horses and take them for a ride?"

Joe led the couple to two of Megan's well-broken horses. As he untied the first horse, he asked. "Where are you from?"

"We're from Hoboken, New Jersey. And you?"

"Brooklyn."

The trio chuckled. Joe remarked, "We've got to show these Texans how to ride."

"Sounds good."

The hour-long ride was along a dry streambed. The riders saw a flock of turkeys, an armadillo, and two feral pigs. The young man asked Joe, "How did these animals get here?"

Joe laughed. "They walked."

The young man's face turned red—he chuckled. "Ask a silly question, get a silly answer."

"I'm sorry, just kidding. The turkeys and armadillo are native to this area. The pigs are descended from domestic pigs who escaped; the ranchers and farmers don't care for them."

Joe pointed out the different bushes and trees. He commented, "Just one hour, and you two are sitting the horses very well."

The young couple tried to give Joe a tip.

He smiled and said, "Thank you, but no. I enjoyed your company. Come back and see us again."

After the couple pulled away, Megan said, "Except for the accent, you sounded like a real Texan."

Joe smiled and said, "This accent ain't goin' away."

He turned to look at her. "You know a lot about me, but I know very little about you."

"I know." She threw her arms around him. Joe was startled but recovered and held her tight. As she relaxed her hold on him, she smiled and said, "Come with me tomorrow while I exercise my birds."

Chapter 69

BIRDS OF PREY

The following day, Megan picked up Joe mid-morning. She had a portable rack in the back seat; two raptors sat on a perch with hoods covering their heads. Joe slid into the passenger's seat. "Are those birds going to stay put?"

Megan chuckled. "They don't like Italian food."

"Yo birdies, I'm Italian!"

Megan laughed and put the truck in gear. "We're going to Kyle's place above Palo Duro Canyon."

Joe decided to jump right in. He asked, "I think you know most of my history. Is there anything you'd like to talk about?"

"I thought you gave up chasing bad guys. This last episode with the drug dealers was a surprise. One, you didn't confide in me, and two, it seems you still want to be in law enforcement."

"I'm sorry I didn't talk to you about what I was doing. I didn't go looking for it." Joe told of his initial encounters with Bump Stock. "I didn't know the man I shot during the bank robbery in Brooklyn was the brother of a powerful drug lord." He told her how the DEA had captured all the hit squad members and that the drug lord was on the run. "I have no desire to be back in law enforcement. What I want to do is figure out how we can have a life together."

He hesitated, then continued, "I know practically nothing about you."

Megan waited for Joe to finish. "My life is full of complications. You already know my father got killed in action; my mother died not long after from a combination of cancer and grief. As you know, we moved around a lot with the military. I went to six different schools by the time I graduated high school." She paused and took a deep breath. "When I was 19, I married a lieutenant I met at Fort Bragg—he was a paratrooper. Unfortunately, the marriage didn't last; when he drank, he was abusive." A smile briefly crossed her face. "One night, he took a swing at me. He was so drunk I punched him and knocked him out. That was the last straw. I packed up, left, and filed for a divorce."

She smiled at Joe. "We brought the birds to exercise them. We'll talk more after I get the birds set."

Joe scratched his head. "I promise never to hit you. But you have to agree not to knock me out."

Megan laughed, "That's a deal. Now help me set up the birds."

"Sure, tell me what to do."

"Not a problem."

The falcon perched on her padded arm, its long nails digging into the padded sleeve. With her free hand, Megan removed the bird's hood. She tossed the falcon into the air and swung a lure in a wide circle; the bird circled, and Megan's shrill whistle brought the raptor diving toward her. She threw a piece of raw meat on the ground. The bird devoured it. Then it flew to her gloved hand and ate the treat held between the thumb and forefinger of the gauntlet. After the bird finished eating, Megan placed a hood over the bird's eyes. "Okay, girl, time to get back on your perch."

Megan said, "It's time for lunch." She took a picnic basket from the truck and spread a blanket on the ground. "Close your eyes, and pretend you're eating in Paris."

Joe joined her on the quilt and selected a sandwich and a bottle of water. "Time for you to fill me in on your background." Joe asked, "Where did you learn how to handle these birds?"

"Well, it's not as exciting as your story." She paused. "After my divorce, I applied to Colorado State University. My goal was to become a forest ranger.

"The school had falcons as mascots. One professor was a master falconer, and I became interested. He trained me. Falconry requires a state license, and Professor Roman sponsored me before I took the state exam."

"I didn't know there is a license required."

Megan nodded. "After you get your apprentice license, you can trap a raptor for training. My first bird was a peregrine. It was the same breed as the one we've just worked." She stroked the falcon. "This bird I've had for two years. I'll probably release it this summer."

★ ★ ★

That afternoon, they drove to the Night Owl Café. Megan placed the birds into their separate cages.

Rowdy called out, "Megan, come up front and have a latte."

"Joe's with me."

"Bring him too!"

Joe couldn't resist. "Do real cowboys drink lattes?"

Rowdy, never lost for words, said, "Unlikely cowboys do."

The three sat at their favorite table. Rowdy asked, "How was your day?"

Megan responded, "The birds did great."

Joe spoke, "We had a lot to talk about."

Rowdy folded his hands on the table. "You both have complicated histories, but you can't live in the past." He tapped his thumbs. "I know that as well as anyone. If you see a chance for something more, you have to go for it."

Chapter 70

BISON CAFÉ

Joe knew he needed a change. Now that he wasn't in law enforcement, he realized the gunsmith store had gotten him into situations he wanted to avoid.

In the first week of June, there was torrential rainfall. Megan called Joe and said, "I'm not going to open the stable until the ground absorbs the rain."

Joe asked, "Do you think your hired hand can see to the horses for a few days?"

"Sure. Why?"

"I've been thinking about our future. I'd like to take a day trip to continue our discussion."

"Okay. Yes, we need to do this."

"I'll pick you up tomorrow. I have a surprise for you." After he ended the call, Joe thought, *I want to spend the rest of my life with Megan.*

Megan slid into the passenger seat. "You said you had a surprise?"

"You'll see."

They drove south on the interstate and exited at Tulia. Megan said, "This is where Kenneth Wyatt has a studio."

"That's our first stop."

The Wyatt Studio on the Comanche Trail looked like a home. Joe parked in the small parking lot. As they entered the front door, an elderly man extended his hand. "Welcome, I'm Kenneth Wyatt."

Joe smiled. "I was here last week, but I think you were away."

"I was at my Ruidoso gallery. My assistant told me a Mediterranean-looking man with a northern accent stopped by."

He looked at Megan. "What's your name?" Megan introduced herself.

Joe asked, "Is it okay if we look around?"

"Of course. If you have any questions, don't hesitate."

Megan and Joe walked upstairs to the main gallery. The walls displayed art dedicated to cowboys and cattle. Scattered around the gallery were western-themed bronze sculptures.

Megan commented, "I've never seen a collection like this. That scene titled 'Room at the Top' reminds me of Kyle and you when we were gathering cattle in the canyons."

"That's what I thought. Do you think Kyle and Britta would like the painting?"

She nodded. "They already have a collection of art but nothing like this."

Kenneth walked up the stairs and approached them. "See anything you can't live without?"

"I want to buy my friend a painting." He pointed at "Room at the Top." Joe looked at the price tag and asked, "Does the price include the frame?"

"Yes, sir."

"I'll take it."

"Who are you buying this for?"

"Kyle Mitchell."

"He's the rancher in Canyon." Wyatt continued, "I've known the family for years. Give me a minute. I want to inscribe a message to Kyle."

Megan held the door as Joe loaded the portrait in the rear seat of the pickup.

Megan commented, "That's a nice gift."

"Kyle's one of my oldest friends. He got me to move down here." Joe continued, "Are you hungry?"

"I could eat."

"Good, we're heading to Quitaque; there's a great restaurant there." Quitaque was an old cowboy town south of Caprock Canyons State Park.

They drove out of town, heading east on Route 86. A bridge crossed a dry streambed that was named Tule Creek. Megan said, "This is the place where the cavalry slaughtered the Native Americans' ponies."

Joe remarked, "There's a lot of history around here." They drove past several ranches. "This is cattle country. There's some farming, mostly planted with feed for the cattle in the winter." They crested a hill overlooking the extension of the Palo Duro Canyon system.

"There's the restaurant." He pointed to the Bison Café.

They sat at a table under a sizeable wrought-iron chandelier attached to a paneled ceiling. A waitress approached and asked Joe and Megan what they'd like to drink. Joe looked at Megan and said, "I'd recommend the raspberry iced tea."

Megan smiled at the waitress and said, "Make it two." She slowly scanned the restaurant. The paintings on the wall portrayed western and religious themes.

The waitress asked Joe, "Were you here last week with Cowboy?"

Joe blushed as he asked, "You remembered me?"

She handed them menus as she remarked, "Cowboy is famous. His family has lived around here since ranchers and homesteaders settled the area."

As they looked at the menus, Megan asked, "What were you and Cowboy doing this far south?"

"It's a surprise."

Megan's eyes widened at the plate before her. "Am I supposed to eat this in one sitting?"

The server remarked, "It's not unusual for customers to get takeout boxes for half of the order. Anything else?"

"No, thank you. Let's eat."

As they were leaving the restaurant, Megan asked, "What's next?"

"You'll see."

Chapter 71

FULL CIRCLE

The Flat Top Mountain Ranch

Joe headed south on FM 1065. The road was flat and straight until it turned, descended, and crossed Los Lingos Creek. Megan noted, "I think I've heard of this creek before."

Joe said, "I read the book *Empire of the Summer Moon*. The comancheros camped here and traded with the Comanches, Spanish traders from Santa Fe, fur trappers, and buffalo hunters."

The red bed of the river coursed through striated cliffs. Mesquite and cedar trees bracketed the trail by the river. "Follow the river to Los Lingos Falls, and you can see where the trading took place."

Megan was captivated by the rough beauty of the land. Quitaque Creek meandered under an overpass. As they crested a rise, Megan exclaimed, "Look at that flat top mountain. Isn't this Cowboy's ranch?"

"Yes. We visited the ranch with Cowboy but only spent the day, not much time. Remember?"

Megan nodded her head.

Joe's lips curved into a smile. At the crossroads with FM 97, Joe turned right and drove about a half-mile. They turned off the road at the iron gate with the sign: *Flat Top Mountain Ranch*. Joe parked in front of the entrance gate, removed the lock, and opened the gate. As he drove through the gate, Megan asked, "Where did you get the key?"

"From Cowboy."

"Joe, what did you do?"

"I came back and learned more about the ranch from Cowboy. It's been in his family for many years; there are about twenty owners—descendants from the family that originally bought the land from Charles Goodnight." As the road wove through the property, they passed flat areas cleared of brush. Joe pointed out areas that were perfect for livestock. After passing through another gate, the road followed the fence line. A steep drop-off led to the cabin in a cleared area, which Megan recognized from their first visit. They parked and headed for the cabin.

Several lawn chairs sat on the three-sided porch. Joe suggested, "Let's sit for a while."

"Is it okay?"

"I got permission from Cowboy."

They enjoyed the gurgling stream that flowed into the acre-sized pond. Cooing doves and the chirping of bluebirds were the only sounds. Megan smiled. "This place is almost paradise. I loved it the first time we came here."

"That's the same thing I thought." Joe reached out and held Megan's hand. "This would be a great place to release your falcons." He shifted his chair and looked into her eyes. "I moved to Texas to get away from law enforcement. But unfortunately, the gun shop appears to be a magnet for trouble. So I've told Rachel that I'm going to close the shop. As it turns out, that fits well with her plans. She told me Brad and Sue want to expand their art studios and need my space."

A light breeze ruffled the cottonwood trees; fluffy white cotton floated toward the lovers. A small flock of turkeys emerged from the streambed and strutted toward them. Joe said, "I've made a deal with Cowboy to purchase the place."

She squeezed his hand and turned to face him. "It would be a perfect setting for a wedding."

Chapter 72

JUST DO WHAT YOU'RE TOLD

One evening after he and Megan had talked, Joe called Kyle. "Are you and Britta at home?"

"Where do you think we'd be?"

"I need to talk to you."

"Well, come on by."

Joe hung up, locked his door, and drove his truck to Kyle's ranch.

Britta greeted him. "Hey Joe, how are you?"

"I've got some news to share with both of you."

"Come in. Kyle's having a beer on the back porch."

His friend motioned him to a chair and handed him a can of beer. "What's goin' on?"

Joe fidgeted and sipped his beer. Then, finally, Britta asked, "Is this about Megan?"

"Yes." Joe told them of his decision to close the gunsmith store and that he had purchased Cowboy's home place. Joe went on, "Did you know his name is Tiberius Jones?"

Kyle raised his eyebrows. "No."

"Cowboy was named after his ancestor who originally settled here." Joe continued, "And he had to sign the bill of sale with his real name."

Kyle's smile broadened. "I can't wait to call him Tiberius!"

Joe shook his head. "Not a good idea."

Joe clasped his hands in front of his chin. "After I drove Megan around the place, I mentioned that it would be a good area to release her birds. She agreed and also thought it would be a good place for a wedding."

Kyle asked, "Whose wedding?"

Britta frowned at Kyle and turned to Joe. "We've been hoping you and Megan would get together. She's a great gal!" She clasped her hands together. "This is going to be fun."

Kyle remarked, "Now you've cranked her up."

Britta could hardly wait to share the news. All of Joe and Megan's friends were happy for them.

The ladies met with Megan to plan the wedding.

As the chosen day arrived, Joe asked Britta, "You and Megan made all these plans. What am I supposed to do?"

She smiled and said, "Show up."

Kyle said, "Just do what you're told."

Chapter 73

THE WEDDING DAY

The day of the wedding arrived. Joe and Kyle stood waiting on Kyle's patio. The prairie grass waved in a gentle breeze. The door opened, and Willy Simmons walked over to his friends. The three friends embraced in a group hug. Joe asked, "How did you get roped into this?"

"Britta and Shirley have burned up the telephone lines planning all this. They've been up since sunrise working."

"Why didn't anyone tell me?"

"The women wanted to surprise you."

Joe asked, "Any more surprises?"

Kyle smiled and said, "You'll see."

Britta, Sue, Rachel, and Shirley exited the house. Joe exclaimed, "They've all got the same dress. How in the world did those women pull this off?"

Willy responded, "Don't ask."

Shirley escorted the local minister to the newly assembled arbor. She shooed the men to their place. The sound of Bach's "Jesu, Joy of Man's Desiring" floated through the air. The patio door opened, and Megan looked stunning in her A-line, floor-length chiffon dress. A wreath of flowers circled her head. Rowdy and Mrs. Milstead escorted Megan and stood to the side. Megan smiled. Joe couldn't take his eyes off her.

The minister pronounced Megan and Joe man and wife. Then, as they turned around, a burst of applause greeted them.

The guests entered the family room. They were greeted by a table full of hors d'oeuvres and a bartender ready to fill drink orders.

An attractive dark-haired young lady walked over to Rowdy and took his hand. Megan ran to the young lady and threw her arms around her. Mrs. Milstead said to Joe, "That's Rowdy's high school sweetheart. Megan knew her in school."

Deputy Williams approached Joe. He had a young lady on his arm. Megan explained, "This is my niece from Wyoming."

The sun was setting as the last guest said goodbye. Britta, Shirley, and Megan sat in the living room. Britta noted, "Joe's hands weren't shaking."

Shirley commented, "It took Willy's hands ten years to stop."

Megan smiled and said, "All the old vets have problems and need understanding."

Shirley remarked, "At some point, Joe's going to open up to you about his wartime experiences—just listen."

Britta nodded in agreement. "Let's give the men some time alone."

Kyle laughed as Willy joked about their former captain. Joe remarked, "When you were on point, if you so much as scratched your nose, he'd dive for the ditch."

Kyle commented, "It's time for some rotgut bourbon." He walked to the bar, poured three glasses halfway with whiskey, added ice, and topped off the glasses with water.

The men sat and reminisced about their tours of duty. Their laughter echoed through the house.

Britta opened the patio door. "Time to call it a night."

In unison, the men answered, "It's a night." They laughed all the more.

Willy remarked, looking at Kyle, "That's what you said to the MPs in Panama. We got to spend the night in the brig."

Kyle told Joe that Willy was going to be around for a week or two. "Let's get together again." He looked at Megan. "Where are you two going on your honeymoon?"

Megan answered, "The Flat Top Mountain Ranch."

ACKNOWLEDGMENTS

Denise, my wife, labored through my writer's block, misspellings, and grammar and punctuation errors. She patiently listened to my ramblings about the characters and structure of the book. Without her, this book would not have happened.

Aloha Publishing designed a book I'm proud to call mine. I created this book with the help and guidance of Jennifer Regner, editor, and Maryanna Young, publisher. These ladies have suffered through three edits and polished the manuscript to a finished product.

Thanks to my son, Bernard Doucette, who graciously served as beta reader of my first draft. His comments enriched the book.

ABOUT THE AUTHOR

James E. Doucette (Jim) grew up in Bedford-Stuyvesant, Brooklyn, New York. He joined the U.S. Navy in 1957 and completed high school and college at night. Jim worked for several telecommunications companies until 1983. In 1984, he founded Cablevision of Texas, constructed or purchased over four hundred cable television systems, and bought a telephone installation company and a home security service.

In 1990, he purchased the First National Bank of Lockney and added four other banks during the next eight years. He began selling his businesses in 1998 and retired in 1999.

Jim and his wife, Denise, live on a ranch in Floyd County, Texas. At the beginning of 2019, they sold the last of their cows. Today, they rent the grazing rights to local cattlemen. They have been blessed with three sons, a daughter recently deceased, and four grandchildren. Jim wrote his first book, *The Not So Great American Novel,* a memoir, in 2015. He published *Flat Top Mountain Ranch: The Beginning* in 2019. His other published books are *Stealing Fire*, which was republished as *Russia's Biggest Hack,* and *The Last Assassination.* He also contributed to the writing of *Witnesses to the Crucifixion: Stories of Redemption and the Healing Power of Jesus,* authored by Ricky Carstensen.

THE WORKS OF
JAMES E. DOUCETTE

Jim started writing as therapy a number of years ago. His first book was *The Not So Great American Novel,* a memoir of his life in business.

That title was an attempt at humor—and the literary majors in his writing group immediately jumped on this with no humor whatsoever because **a biography is not a novel.** Okay, then.

His first two novels, *Stealing Fire* (which was republished as *Russia's Biggest Hack*) and *The Last Assassination,* are historical fiction. Many of the fictitious events he invented for these novels came true—so he made fake news before anyone heard of it.

The Flat Top Mountain Ranch: The Beginning is also historical fiction but it's doubtful the real world will imitate his imagination in this one.

The Unlikely Cowboy takes you back to the Flat Top Mountain Ranch in the contemporary world. The protagonists end up in West Texas when their worlds in Colorado and New York fall apart. Those pesky characters sometimes take him to places he never imagined.

If you have any comments about this book or any of his books, please contact Jim via email at james_doucette@yahoo.com. He promises to answer you.

His books are available on Amazon.com.

Printed in Great Britain
by Amazon

31628308R00182